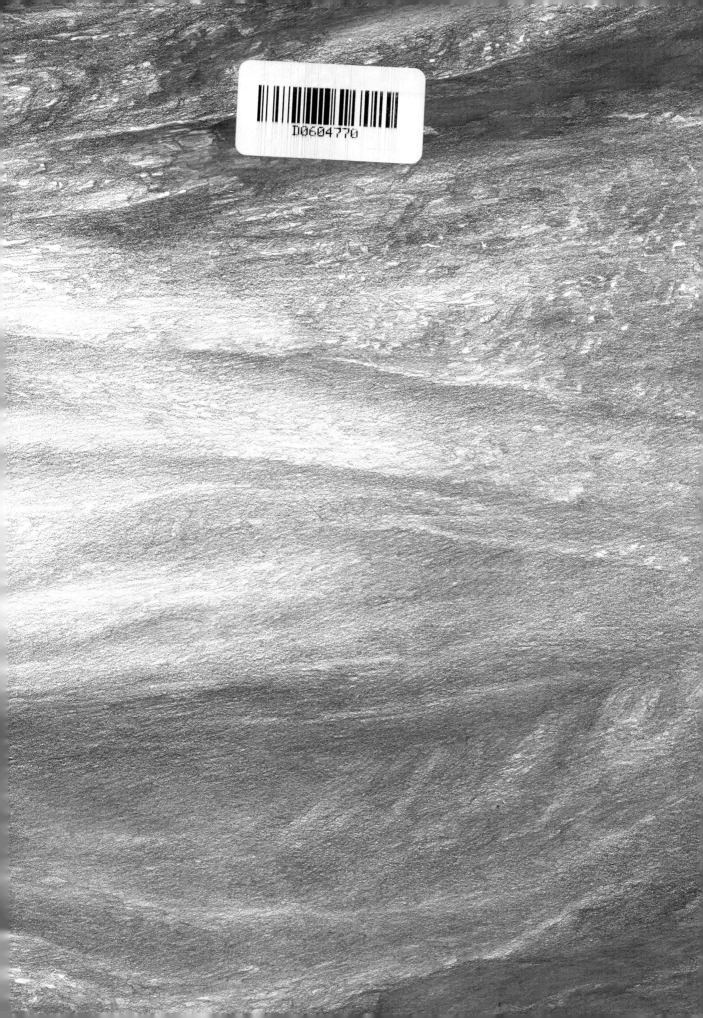

MERLIN DREAMS

MERLIN DREAMS

MERLIN DREAMS

PETER DICKINSON
illustrated by
ALAN LEE

Delacorte
Press

Published by Delacorte Press
The Bantam Doubleday Dell Publishing Group, Inc.
666 Fifth Avenue, New York, New York 10103

First published in Great Britain by Victor Gollancz Ltd

Text copyright © Peter Dickinson 1988
Illustrations copyright © Alan Lee 1988

The trademark Delacorte Press® is registered
in the U.S. Patent and Trademark Office.

Library of Congress Cataloging-in-Publication Data
Dickinson, Peter, 1927–
    Merlin Dreams / Peter Dickinson; illustrated by Alan Lee.
        p.   cm.
    Summary: Nine stories of blood, magic, and fabulous creatures,
set in the framing device of dreams coming to the enchanted wizard
Merlin as he lies imprisoned under a great stone.
    ISBN 0-440-50067-2
    1. Merlin (Legendary character) – – Juvenile fiction.   2. Fantastic
fiction, English.   [1. Merlin (Legendary character) – – Fiction.
2. Fantasy.   3. Short stories.]   I. Lee, Alan, ill.   II. Title.
PZ7.D562Me 1988
[Fic] – – dc19   88.3985
                                                                                CIP
                                                                                AC

Manufactured in Hong Kong
November 1988
10 9 8 7 6 5 4 3 2 1

"Then it happened that Merlin began to dote on a damsel named Nenyve. He would not let her alone, and had to be with her all the time. And she made herself pleasant to him until she had learnt of him all kinds of things she wanted. He was besotted with her . . . but she was always wary of him, and wished to be free of him, for she was afraid of him because he was a devil's son, but she could not be rid of him by any means. Then Merlin showed her a rock that contained a great wonder beneath it. By her cunning she persuaded Merlin to go under the rock to let her know of the marvels there, but then she worked a spell so that he could never come out for all his skill. So she departed and left him."

from *The Tale of King Arthur* by Sir Thomas Malory

They stood on bare moor. No house between horizon—no, not even a path. They might have been the only people in all Britain. She was young, still, watchful. He was not old, but haggard—cheeks hollow, bloodshot eyes deep sunk, skin seamed and dead-looking. There was a froth of spittle at the corner of his mouth.

A shudder shook him. He closed his eyes and held out a hand towards her. She did not move for a moment but stood tense and deciding, like the keeper of a big and dangerous animal, who has to guess at every moment whether the animal's training will hold or its wildness break loose. There were bruises on her neck and shoulder which reminded her that yesterday she had guessed wrong.

Despite that she stepped closer and took his hand. The shuddering did not stop. She led him like a blind man towards the rock.

It was a long, dark hummock rising from the sour turf like the back of a broaching whale. Four fifths of its mass lay below ground-level. She put the hand she was holding against it, then took his other hand and helped it find the rock. Still with his eyes shut he patted the grainy surface, fumbling to and fro, until his stubby bear-like hands seemed to choose their exact spot and then somehow suck themselves almost into the rock, limpet-close, so that it would have needed immense force to drag them free. Slowly the shuddering died away. He rested for a long while with his head bowed and his weight on his arms, leaning against the rock.

She stood close, watching him all the time, and was ready when, without warning, he dropped. She caught him—the exhausted body was light as dry bone—and eased him down to sit with his back against the rock. She looked at the sky and checked that rain-clouds were clearing— he had said they would—then fetched the bundle she had carried across the moor. Most of its weight was firewood, because they had known there would be none on this treeless upland.

She built the fire slowly. As she settled each log in place she held her hands over it in a gesture of blessing and whispered one of the Secret Names. Sometimes she shivered a little. The forces that had so ravaged him were alive in her too, infecting her like a disease. One day, perhaps, her face would be as haggard as his and her body be shaken by the same storms—or perhaps not, for she would never be able to know and endure a thousandth part of what he had known and endured. Nobody would, not ever again.

When the fire was built she prepared a small lamp, then took a fireboard and tinder and a pointed stick. She twisted the stick rapidly to and fro between her palms until the tinder started to smoulder with friction round the point. She blew as she twisted until she had a spark, from which she could light a twist of dry grass and set the lamp going. He could have lit the lamp with a touch of his fingers. She could have done the same with rather more effort. But what they were here to do had to be kept clean of such trivial magics.

When everything was ready she sat beside him and eased his body down so that she could lay his head in her lap. With an old bone comb she smoothed his hair and beard until he woke.

He opened his eyes to stare up past her at a rainwashed evening sky, pale and clear. His crusted lips smiled. He rose and stretched, looking round the empty moor. In a clear voice he spoke to hill and sky as though they were alive and his equals. Then he squatted down beside the woman. She had gone very pale and was trembling, but he stroked her head until she gathered herself together, drew back her shoulders and repeated in a low voice the lesson he had taught her. It lasted some time and had to be exact in every word. He nodded when she had finished. She was still pale but had stopped trembling.

Now he undressed completely and went and sat cross-legged by the fire she had built, looking across it towards the rock. She used the lamp to light the straw. As soon as the logs had caught she dribbled a handful of dried leaves onto the flames. They burnt with a pale, bitter smoke which he leaned forward to breathe in great lungfuls. Then he sat erect, muttering Names.

Suddenly his eyes rolled upward in their sockets till only the bloodshot whites showed. His body juddered as though invisible talons had gripped it and were battering it to and fro. He wailed like a cat. Something whipped against the woman's side, knocking her half over, but she staggered clear and stood watching while he mastered the forces he had summoned and sucked them whirling into his body. Twice more she judged her moment and came close enough to dribble more leaves onto the fire, to make the strange smoke for him to breathe. Twice more he juddered and wailed— only now it was the whole moor that seemed to be shaking. The woman shook with it and staggered to and fro, barely keeping her footing. Only two things were still—the flame from the fire, steady as a sword-blade, and the man's body where he sat staring blind-eyed towards the shuddering rock.

He rose, like smoke, effortless, weightless. He was larger now and stood broad-shouldered. He stretched his arms wide. The air around him glowed and heat beamed from his body. He spoke in a ringing voice, each syllable solid as a pebble. His voice went into the rock. The rock spoke back. It groaned. It complained aloud. But it rose slowly from its bed, heaving the turf aside, tilting upwards until a dark slit appeared between earth and stone. The man walked forward, going straight through the fire without displacing an ember. He bent, crooked his fingers below the rock, then straightened, raising his arms over his head, holding those thousands of tons above him. Without looking back or feeling for footholds he walked down into the darkness. Behind him the rock sank slowly into the wounded earth.

At once the woman ran forward and with bare feet stamped out the flames, which did not burn her. She fetched a clay pot and scooped ashes and embers into it, then walked in a wide circle all round the rock, tossing the ashes to left and right like a sower of wheat. That done, she climbed to the top of the rock and chanted the words he had taught her, crying them clear-voiced to north, east, south, west, and north again. As she spoke the torn earth regathered itself round the rock, the crevices closed and the turf grew close as a mat. The evening air shimmered with departing energies. It was nightfall by the time she had ended.

She climbed down, stooping with exhaustion, and packed her bundle together. As she strapped it across her shoulders she looked round the dark, empty arena, sighing. Last of all she bent and kissed the rock, then walked with weary steps across the moor. There was a half-moon high, a moon that he would never see again, except in dreams.

Later, back among people, she told them openly what she had done. They believed her but did not understand. He had been so huge a figure in their lives, for so long. Then he had chosen this girl, picked her out from a group singing round a well-head when she was ten years old, and started to teach her some of his knowledge and his power. In the end (she said so herself) she had used that knowledge and power to bind him below a rock. So they decided he must have been besotted with her, and she had led him on for the sake of what he could teach her, and when she had learnt all she could she had coaxed from him a spell he could not undo and had used it to get rid of him. So they worked it out, for ordinary people imagine ordinary things. Even so, they were puzzled. He had foreknowledge among his other powers. He had told many dooms, all true. Surely he must have known his own. Had he then, somehow, chosen?

She left them to their supposing and went north. Later she used her power to rescue a man she loved from an enchantment, and married him. No more is known of her. She too seems to have chosen her doom. It was to become like other people, ordinary.

And he? Many years later a fighter claimed that he had found the actual rock and spoken with the man beneath it, and the man had told him nothing could release him. So, sometimes, it seems, he was awake. Mostly he lay deep in the inward darkness he had chosen. But sometimes, between waking and sleeping, he would dream . . .

The faint whisper of water, where rain on the moor above feels its way downward. Woken by the sound the drowsy mind senses the flow, how the veins of water runnel together and become a stream under the moor, welling out miles away at a chill spring.

Memory condenses like a dew-drop. Deep in that clear globe a thing once seen.

A certain holy pool, one of many such, worshipped by its tribe. An ash-tree leaned over the water, reflected in its surface. Close by the grey trunk stood a man, the priest of the pool, fed and honoured by the tribe, but the marks of his priesthood were not the long white robe or the mistletoe-garland, they were the sword at his belt and the round shield on his shoulder. A killer-priest. On the door-posts of his hut five heads were nailed, men who had come to challenge him for the priesthood, and lost, and become sacrifices to the goddess of the pool.

And now there came a sixth. A stranger, young and tall, hair smeared with white clay, shield at shoulder, sword at belt, striding to the ash-tree, breaking a branch. Like a wolf at a buck the priest leaped towards him, and the swords clashed in the stillness . . .

But before the fight is ended the remembering mind looses its hold and swims down towards darkness. Memory quivers, like reflections in rippled water . . . and now it is changed into dream, all changed. The pool is a river with a foaming ford. The guardian sits on his horse, armoured, plumed, lance in hand, waiting for the stranger-knight, the challenge . . .

KNIGHT ERRANT

HE long harsh note of the trumpet echoed from moss-streaked walls and dwindled among turrets. In leaking attics (it was a wet April) servants stirred. Before the last echoes died the trumpet blared again. Men-at-arms woke swearing. Again the note of danger.

By the third time only two people in Castle Gall were still asleep. Sir Tremalin snorted face-down on his bed, where his servants had dumped him last night, still in his clothes and still half-drunk. The boy Dai lay curled by the fire in the hall, worn out with trudging through the forest, unwilling to face the day after the grim disappointment at the journey's end. Everyone else—not many, for Sir Tremalin paid poor wages when he paid at all—jumped from where they slept, ran to a window, and stared down into the courtyard. Under a watery April sun they saw the trumpeter in his bright tabard, the six knights in shining steel, forty foot-soldiers in good chain-mail, and over them all, flapping in the brisk breeze, the banner of the King.

Feet scuttled on floors, hands groped into hiding-places for small hoards, gathered from years of thieving, all but the two sleepers scuttled for one of the castle's bolt-holes. But the six knights had laid their plans well. The exits were guarded, and the escapers were rounded up and taken to wait in the courtyard. Then the herald put his trumpet to his lips and blew three more blasts. This time both sleepers woke.

Dai pushed himself up, groaning, and looked round the empty hall, with its smoke-blacked rafters, its ramshackle furniture, and the dank rushes that strewed its floor mingled with the rotting spillage of old meals. He groaned again, remembering last evening, Sir Tremalin grinning in his tilted chair as Dai blurted his message, the drunken servants guffawing at the hopelessness of it.

Sir Tremalin too sat up groaning, and went on groaning as he groped to the window. Standing well back so that he would not be seen from below he looked down into the courtyard. Six knights. Foot-soldiers. A herald. The King's banner. His own servants standing roped at the back . . . then the bolt-holes must be blocked. Hide? His servants knew the places. Face the knights in combat? If he had to, in the end, but . . . Wait! That fool boy with his idiot message—where was he? Not in the courtyard yet. Quick, before he went whining to one of these noble knights . . .

Dai was struggling to lift the big beam that barred the main door when Sir Tremalin came up behind him, caught him by the ear and spun him round.

"Well, boy," he purred, "I have slept on your message. I have thought long and deep on it. I hereby accept your plea and take your quest on me."

Dai stared at the twitching pale face, the blue and bristly chin, the small eyes, bloodshot but sharp.

"You?" he whispered, appalled.

"Me and none else," said Sir Tremalin. "Do you accept me as your Knight and Champion, on behalf of your fair city? Say 'I do'."

"I . . . I . . ."

"That's enough. Now come with me. Stand at my side. Look happy."

Sir Tremalin heaved the beam up, swung the door open, pulled his shoulders square and lurched out to face the knights. They moved into an arc to meet him, gazing down from their tall chargers. The herald lowered his trumpet and came forward.

13

"Good morning, gentle sirs," said Sir Tremalin. He managed to look pleased, though still not pleasant.

"You are that false knight, Tremalin, of Castle Gall?" said the herald.

"I am Sir Tremalin and this is my castle."

The herald unrolled a parchment and started to read it out.

"By order of the High King, given at his court in Camlo. Whereas the dastard knight Tremalin hath by his many evil deeds brought into dishonour our noble institution of knighthood, and whereas . . ."

Sir Tremalin reached forward, took the parchment and pretended to read it—something he could not have done even sober. He smiled up at the knights.

"A challenge?" he said. "Each of you valiant sirs in turn? To the death? Or else be hanged from my own battlements?"

(Though he could not read, he knew the form well enough.)

The central knight answered.

"From the King's own lips we have the order. And I, Sir Galavail, will undertake the first encounter and prove upon your body your foul misdeeds."

"And I, Sir Burdac, will undertake the second, should Sir Galavail not succeed," said the knight beside him, smiling at the unlikeliness of that being the case. The other four spoke in turn, each giving his name and issuing his challenge. They were all famous fighters, heroes of great adventures. Sir Tremalin heard them out, nodding affably.

"And I, Sir Tremalin," he answered, "would gladly meet these challenges and prove on your six bodies, though against all odds, that the tales which have come to the ears of the King are all false slanders. Unhappily that cannot be. I have this very morning undertaken a quest."

"You?" cried Sir Galavail. "A quest, false knight?"

Sir Tremalin rubbed his hands together and bowed his head.

"I and none other," he said. "Unworthy though I am I have undertaken as perilous a quest as could be known. I go to fight with a knight who rides invisible. Speak, boy. Tell these noble knights your message."

Dai glanced at him—flabby, greasy, trembling with drink. He looked at the other six knights, noble and hardened warriors on their great horses. If only one of them . . .

"I bear a message from the city called Beausoleil," he said. "We are oppressed by an evil lord, a knight who rides invisible. He that shall slay this knight and rescue our city we will accept as our good lord to rule us and guard us as long as he shall live."

"Where is this city?" said Sir Galavail.

"Beyond the Great Forest, my lord. The road is perilous. In the forest of old time there laired a great dragon, from whose presence all the waters

14

of the forest, except two wells, are poisoned. These wells are guarded by knights, servants of our dread lord. Last of all there is a river, with a ford which is guarded by our dread lord himself. There is no other road through the forest. Whoever would come to our city of Beausoleil must fight all three."

"You understand, good sirs," purred Sir Tremalin. "If one of you were to kill me, then for the honour of knighthood one of you must also undertake the quest the boy brings. Knights who guard wells you have fought often, but a knight who rides invisible . . . ? Moreover, this quest is mine. The boy was told to demand help from the first knight he met."

The six knights glanced at each other, withdrew a little way and muttered together. When they came back Sir Galavail spoke.

"Boy," he said, "you are assured there is no other path through the forest?"

"None is known, my lord. The poison of the old dragon makes all other ways too dangerous."

"How did you yourself come? Why did your city send a child?"

"My lord, my grandmother is a Wise Woman. She dreamed a dream that the time was ready for a messenger to go and ask for help against our dread lord. The knights at the wells would have stopped a grown man or woman, but our lord makes us take out food to them. My father hid me in a basket and carried me to the well of the Green Knight. From there I stole away. It was in my grandmother's dream that I must go to the first knight I met."

"Very good," said Sir Galavail. "Now, false knight, hear our doom. You shall go on this quest. We will set you on the road into the forest and we will then guard that road till you return. When you do so you will bring the boy with you, as a witness that you have fulfilled your quest. If you come without him, be assured that we will hang you as a false knight from the nearest tree."

They set out before noon, travelling over poor fields and then across a dreary waste. The dark mass of the forest rolled away on their right as they rode north. The sudden April rains swept over it. That night when they camped Sir Tremalin was guarded like a prisoner. Late next morning he rode into the forest. Dai followed behind on the pack-horse. It was very silent under the trees. Not a bird sang in the height of spring.

Sir Tremalin's armour was blotched with rust. Its thongs were half perished. Loose rivets rattled at every pace of his lame old charger—the pack-horse was a better animal. At the first curve of the forest track he reined and looked back out of the gloomy green tunnel to where the six knights glittered in the sunlight. Now they were smiling and he was not.

The pack-horse carried food for six days, but water only for two. As the sharp downpours came and went Sir Tremalin inverted his helmet to catch the drips. By mid-afternoon he had collected a few mouthfuls—not enough for a man, let alone a horse. He rode silent and scowling, peering into the tangled dark on either side of the track. Two or three times he took his horse off the road and tried to force a way through the thorny undergrowth, but came back after a few yards, defeated.

"How far to the first well, boy?" he muttered at last.

"I think we will reach it about sunset, my lord."

"What do you know about the fellow who guards it?"

"His name is not known, my lord. He is called the Green Knight."

"A hardy fighter, no doubt."

"They say he has wizard power, my lord. He has beaten many good knights. He takes from each his sword and sends him on to the next well, where the Red Knight waits. He has wizard power also, and has beaten all who come. He takes their lances from them and sends them on weaponless to the ford beneath our city, and there the Knight who Rides Invisible strikes them down and hangs their bodies from his tree."

Sir Tremalin reined, thought, swung his horse round, then stopped and thought again. He turned once more and rode slowly on. Another shower swept over. Drops rattled through the leaves.

"Slower, boy," snarled Sir Tremalin. "We will go by the well in the dark, while this green fool sleeps. There must be pools and streams elsewhere."

"They are all poisoned, my lord. It is the power of the old dragon. And my father told me you cannot pass the wells by night. There is an enchantment."

"It would be so," muttered Sir Tremalin, but still he did not seem to want to ride any faster.

The moon was up and clear between the storm-clouds when suddenly the track came to an end, barred by thickets so dense that a rabbit could hardly have found its way through.

"It is the enchantment, my lord," said Dai. "Look."

He pointed. Between the tree-trunks, perhaps two hundred paces away, shone the orange gleam of a fire.

"That is where the Green Knight keeps his pavilion," said Dai. "We are at the edge of the glade round the well, but by night the forest fills it."

Sir Tremalin dismounted and walked to the edge of the barrier. The moon shone brightly down on the track floor. He studied the grass, and the trees on either side of the track, then led the way back until they were well out of sight of the Green Knight's fire.

They fed and watered the horses and supped off cold food, then wrapped

themselves in blankets and slept on the bare, damp ground. Once when a quick fresh downpour woke him Dai saw that Sir Tremalin had disappeared, but his horse was still there, tethered to a branch. And when Dai was finally woken by the birdless sunrise he saw Sir Tremalin snorting in his blanket on the other side of the track.

Dai knelt and said his prayers. Sir Tremalin sat up and began cursing aloud. He was shivering, and hardly touched his breakfast. While Dai ate Sir Tremalin told him what he wanted.

"My lord, this is not knightly!" said Dai.

"Do you think it knightly to fight with wizard power? Do you think it knightly to strip a fellow of his weapons and send him on to face a knight who rides invisible? You are not a fool, boy. We must do what we can with what we have."

He was still cursing and trembling as Dai helped him into his rusty armour and held the old charger while he mounted. Then Dai stole ahead down the track. At the place where it had seemed to end the night before there was now a grassy smooth glade with a stone well-head at the centre and on the further side a large green tent. A great black horse with fine green trappings stood by the tent, cropping the young grass. Dai knelt behind the last tree, at the very edge of the glade, and waited.

At last Sir Tremalin rode down the track. The moment his horse set hoof in the glade there was a noise like bells ringing from all the trees around. Instantly the flaps of the tent flew aside and a huge knight strode out, all in armour green as leaves. He climbed lightly up his mounting-block and into the saddle, reached for his lance and came thundering over the turf. Sir Tremalin kicked his heels against the ribs of his charger. The poor animal, bewildered at being asked to face an enemy in clean fight, staggered forward.

Now the Green Knight was already at the well-head, coming full tilt, and Sir Tremalin about half way to meet him. Suddenly Sir Tremalin seemed to panic. He dropped his lance, spun his horse round and raced back the way he had come. The horse was much more used to this style of fighting and broke into a gallop, but the Green Knight came faster still. They reached the entrance of the glade with his lance-point two feet from Sir Tremalin's spine.

As the first horse hammered past Dai flung his weight back. The cord he was holding, knotted from the lashings of the pack-horse's load, rose taut across the track. At once he was hauled sprawling as the Green Knight's charger drove into it. The cord was wrenched from his grip, burning his palms. But the charger pecked and fell, sending its rider somersaulting over its neck. He landed with a crash of steel, flat on his back.

Sir Tremalin hauled his own horse violently round. Rapid as an ape he scrambled down and straddled the Green Knight's chest. He flipped off his right gauntlet, felt at his belt and drew out a small dagger with a rounded spike for blade. He had it at the Green Knight's visor when Dai, rushing up from behind, seized his wrist with both hands and tried to haul it away.

"No, no!" he cried. "Let him yield! He will yield!"

Sir Tremalin swore and shook him loose, but at that moment the Green Knight stirred and Sir Tremalin had to drop the dagger in order to throw his whole weight on the big man's arms.

18

"The boy is right," said the Green Knight. "I yield. Loose my helm."

He spread his arms wide and did not struggle as Dai undid the buckles and pulled the helmet clear. The knight's face was pale, but broad and handsome, with clear blue eyes and a gold beard starting to grizzle. He was smiling.

"So I have been beaten by a worse knight than myself," he said.

"You may say that if you choose," said Sir Tremalin.

"I do choose. It is true, and I thank you. Nine years I have held this glade. I was under a spell. Many a better knight than myself I have beaten with the aid of wizard power and sent on to his doom. But now I have been beaten by a worse knight than myself, and the spell is broken. That is why I thank you. Now let me up, and I will do whatever you command me."

"One moment," said Sir Tremalin. "The next well is guarded by a Red Knight, I hear. Is he under the same spell?"

"Yes. The Red Knight is my own brother, but if I rode into his glade he would be forced to fight me."

"How did you come under this spell?"

"My brother and I rode out seeking adventures. We passed through the forest and came to a river by a fine city. The river was in spate and could not be forded, so we rested at a black tent by the crossing. As we sat there, invisible hands brought food to the table. We were hungry and ate. Then suddenly we slept, and when we woke we were under the spell. A voice out of thin air told us its terms. That is all I know. Now let me up."

Grudgingly Sir Tremalin did so. He kept his hand on his sword-hilt until the Green Knight had laid all his weapons aside and taken off his armour. They watered the horses at the well, then ate good food at the Green Knight's tent. Sir Tremalin was careful not to touch anything until he had seen the knight eat from the same dish. He questioned him closely, but learnt no more. In the end he told him to walk to the forest entrance and tell Sir Galavail that he was the King's prisoner, having been vanquished by Sir Tremalin, but not how it was done.

Sir Tremalin did not choose to ride the fine new charger he had won. Instead he made Dai load it with the green armour, food from the Green Knight's store, and all the water they could find containers for. Then they journeyed on. The silence of the forest seemed to grow deeper, as though the wind that swished the tree-tops was blowing in another world. The leaves on the branches, which ought to have been bright with spring and sparkling with the quick-passing showers, instead had a strange dark hue. The air smelt wrong. The horses were nervous at nothing.

About the middle of the afternoon the track widened to another clearing, again with a stone well-head at the centre, but this was a very different place. There was no bright tent, no waiting charger. The earth was sour and dark, without a blade of grass. The trees around were twisted into unnatural shapes, and their leaves were scant and either pale yellow or almost black. Sir Tremalin halted at the edge.

"Why is this, boy?" he croaked.

"My father whispered to me as he carried me through. It is the well where the old dragon used to drink, and where the first lord of our city fought and killed him, and threw his body in the well."

They rode close to the edge of the glade, breathing shallowly of the poisoned air, then on along the further track. That night they slept by its side as before. As they breakfasted next morning Sir Tremalin asked how far it was to the glade where the Red Knight waited.

"We will reach it this morning, I think, my lord," said Dai. "Will you work your trick with the trip-rope?"

"There is the same enchantment, I take it. We may not pass by night?"

"No, my lord."

"That other time, when I rode past you, how far was his spear-tip from my back?"

Dai held his hands apart to show the distance. Sir Tremalin shuddered, swore and shook his head.

The trees around the Red Knight's glade rang their leaves like bells. The Red Knight strode from his tent, swung into his saddle and seized his lance, but he was hardly into his charge when he reined to a halt. A knight in green armour, mounted on a charger with green trappings, was cantering

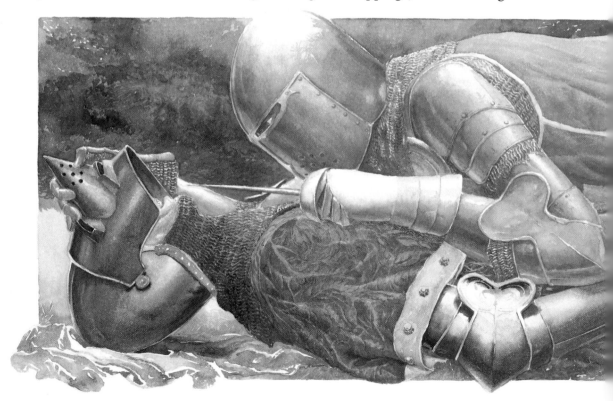

towards him with his right hand raised in greeting. The Red Knight saluted back.

"Is that you, brother?" he cried.

"It is I," clanged the voice inside the green helmet. "My spell is broken. I am free. I come to tell you . . ."

"Yet I must fight you," interrupted the Red Knight. "Brother though you are, the spell compels me. Make ready."

The other knight hesitated.

"If you must, you must," he said. "I rue the day we sat in that cursed tent. But let us at least shake hands and part in friendship."

So they rode together and gripped each other by the elbow in knightly manner. While their hands were still clasped the knight in green raised his left arm and pointed to the other entrance of the glade.

"Look who comes!" he said.

The Red Knight turned his head. Sir Tremalin, in the green armour, flung his full weight against him, pitching him out of his saddle, and leaped down on him as he started to rise, knocking him flat once more. He straddled his chest and held his dagger to the red visor.

"Now yield," he cried. "Yield to a worse knight than yourself."

The moment he heard the words the Red Knight stopped struggling while Dai unlaced his helm. He yielded and rose laughing. Sir Tremalin questioned him about his adventure at the black tent but he knew no more than his brother, so he sent him back to Sir Galavail with the same message. Before they rode on Sir Tremalin made Dai help him change back into his own armour.

"But why, my lord?" said Dai. "The red armour is a fine suit, and you won it by right. Your own . . ."

"It fits me," snarled Sir Tremalin. "I am not ashamed of it."

But he also insisted on riding his own poor nag, and leading the Red Knight's charger with the red armour strapped around its saddle. He seemed in a worse temper than ever. Perhaps the stillness of the woods affected him. He muttered all the time to himself, the same thoughts over and over, often loud enough for Dai to hear.

"He would not fight two knights at a time . . . none guarded the wells before . . . he hoped to fight weaponless men from then on . . . what need of that, when he could come at them invisible . . . ?"

All the time the rain-squalls swept across, darkening the sun for twenty minutes and then moving on, leaving clear skies and pattering branches. They slept by the track as before.

Next morning the forest seemed to thin slightly. A glade would open beside the track and Sir Tremalin would instantly turn aside and explore, only to find his way blocked by thickets.

"It is no use, my lord," said Dai at last. "The river lies before us, a rushing torrent between steep cliffs. If you could find a path you still could not cross. The only passage is at the ford. I can hear the river now."

Sir Tremalin stood and listened. The wind whimpered in the tree-tops, but beneath that note there came a steady mutter, the sound of headlong water dashing itself to foam.

"Are we so near?" he croaked.

"I think so, my lord."

"Keep your voice down! Swear to me that there is no other crossing."

"None, my lord."

"It would be so."

He made Dai tether the horses and prepare food, while he himself stalked cursing round the glade, staring at the sky or the ground as though he thought he might somehow fly or tunnel his way to safety. He ate scowling, then took off all his armour, keeping only his dagger at his belt. He told Dai to follow, went back to the track and stole along its edge in the shadow of the trees.

The mutter of the rapids grew to a boom. Lightness showed beneath the trees, where the forest ended. Sir Tremalin halted, looking to left and right, then picked his way off the track. There was still no easy path but after several false turns he found a way round to the edge of the tree-line a hundred paces or so from the place where the track left the forest. He crawled forward and lay down. Dai settled beside him. Together they gazed out into the open.

"That is Beausoleil, my lord," whispered Dai. "And there is the ford."

The city spread along the hillside beyond the river. It was a fine town, with white walls and turrets, above which a dozen black flags flapped in the wind. To the left the walls rose sheer from a steep cliff with the torrent tumbling white beneath it, but straight ahead the ground dipped to form a wide basin where the river broadened into shallows. The road led through these shallows and out on the further side. Close by the place where it entered the water stood a huge black tent with a black banner over it. Under an awning nearby a black charger nosed into a manger. Nearer still a single oak tree rose. From almost every branch dangled an armoured body, swaying gently in the wind. Nothing else stirred.

Sir Tremalin lay and studied the whole scene, detail by detail. Another shower had fallen and gone before he spoke.

"Go and fetch the Green Knight's horse. Remove all its harness and trappings. Leave only the bare bridle. Not a touch of green, or anything to show whose horse it might be. Lead it along the track to the edge of the wood and whip it across the haunches. Do not yourself be seen."

Dai nodded and crept away. For a long while nothing moved. Then at last the riderless charger shot into the open. Instantly the central tree let out a clanging noise as though the dangling bodies had all been bells, and at the signal the flaps of the black tent whisked apart. The black charger vanished, and all seemed still again. But the riderless horse raised its head and whinnied and was answered by a whinny out of nowhere. Now came the drub of hooves, and a line of hoof-prints began to appear on the rain-softened turf. The riderless horse halted, bewildered, and started to shy away, but a voice spoke out of the air to steady it. Then it too vanished. Only two lines of hoof-prints pocked their way across the turf, going side by side down towards the black pavilion. Then, a few seconds apart, the horses blinked into view, the newcomer tethered to a post. The tent-flaps twitched and closed and the scene was still.

All afternoon Sir Tremalin lay and watched. At dusk he came back to the clearing. He did not speak and ate his food without noticing, then sat picking his broken and blackened teeth with his dagger-point. Next morning, though, he rose early and told Dai to cut branches from trees and bushes, choosing ones which were whippy and strong. He himself worked steadily, bending the cut branches this way and that and then lashing them into a framework. By noon he had finished. He was trembling and could not eat, but in a shaking voice he told Dai exactly what he wanted him to do.

Dai led Sir Tremalin's charger to the point where the road left the forest. On its back rode a figure armed from head to toe in rusty steel, but carrying neither lance nor sword. In the shadow of the trees Dai halted and waited for the signal. He could just see Sir Tremalin crouching by a tree a hundred yards along at the wood's edge. He wore no armour. His shield and lance were propped against the tree. The Red Knight's charger was tethered deeper in the wood behind him. His eyes flickered to and fro, watching the black tent, Dai, the river, the city, the sky.

A squall drove across but Sir Tremalin gave no sign. The sun shone out and still he waited. Again the sky darkened, black as nightfall, and this time as the rain-veil swept towards him Sir Tremalin raised his right arm, waved it twice, and scuttled back into the wood. Dai was leading the old nag into the open when the squall began to drench down so thick that he could hardly see as far as the river, but through the rattle of tumbling drops and the roar of the ford, above the whip of the wind, the bells clanged from the oak tree.

Again the black tent-flaps flew up and again the charger vanished—but this time, not completely. This time, if you looked unflinching, you could just see a something, a difference in the air, like a shadow in the grey-white rainstorm, a place where the water vanished, leaving an empty, silvery, faint bubble.

Dai whipped Sir Tremalin's horse across the haunches to startle it on down the slope. It managed a clumsy canter, with the figure on its back wallowing to and fro. The silvery shadow charged. It came hurtling up through the storm, the shadow of a man on horseback, crouched for the lance-shock. There was something strange about the helmet.

Dai watched, white-faced, seeing for the first time the dread lord of his city, the Knight who Rode Invisible. The shadow came whirling on. Spray shot from the rain-soaked turf where the hoofs tramped. Sir Tremalin's horse, not liking the storm but used to curious loads and so not minding the armoured dummy on its back, slowed from its first rush into the clearing and gazed around, then saw or heard or somehow felt the coming attack and started to wheel away. The shadow's path curved as it followed its target round. At the same moment Sir Tremalin came charging out of the trees. But these moves had altered the game. Now, instead of being able to ambush his enemy from the side, he would have to meet the Knight Invisible face to face.

His face turned chalk white. For an instant he tried to rein his charger back, but this was not the horse he was used to. It was an animal trained for this moment, this deed alone, to put its whole huge weight into the onrush so that its rider might meet his opponent with all the speed and mass that was there. Perhaps if Sir Tremalin had thrown lance and shield aside and hauled full strength on the reins he might have halted the charge —but then what? Waited there, weaponless, armourless, while the Knight Invisible bore down on him? His quick mind must have seen this in the instant, seen that attack was still his only hope. Desperately he clutched lance against side, crouched behind his rusty shield and came driving on.

The shadow-horse too had been trained for the single charge, and perhaps its rider, for all his wizard powers, lacked Sir Tremalin's speed of thought. The shadow seemed to waver a moment, undecided between targets, and in that moment Sir Tremalin was on it. He staggered in the saddle with the shock of impact. His lance vanished from his hand. Suddenly the black-caparisoned horse was there, careering riderless through the rain. A spear flew sideways out of nowhere as the broken butt of another went cartwheeling away. There was the crash of an armoured horseman falling.

Sir Tremalin jumped down, dagger in hand, and looked desperately around, searching the grass for the faint shadow of his enemy. The rain had thinned. In a minute the knight would be fully invisible again, horseless but armed with his sword and deadly as ever.

The rain stopped. Sir Tremalin turned to run for the horses, but then a voice spoke from the ground, an agonised groan, barely words at all.

"I am slain," it said. "Loose the helm. Let me die in clean air."

"Where are you?" croaked Sir Tremalin.

"Here."

Cautiously Sir Tremalin moved over the turf, probing forward with his feet. Suddenly he too vanished, reappeared and vanished again. For a while there was only the scared mutter of his voice and the enemy's answering groan. All at once the two men blinked into being, a strange knight lying on his back, with the broken shaft of Sir Tremalin's spear sticking from the rib-joint of his black armour, and Sir Tremalin himself kneeling by his side but turning away to lay something on the grass. He rose and stood looking down at the wounded man. Dai came and stood beside him.

The knight gazed up at the sky with tired, bleared eyes. His lips were thin and purple, his scant hair pure white, and the skin of his face yellow, blotched, wrinkled with age.

"Who are you?" said Sir Tremalin. "What is your name?"

"I will not tell you my name. It is mine no more. Once it belonged to the best knight in all the world, purest, bravest, strongest—so I thought. Now I have become the worst."

"How? Why?"

"You will soon know. The helm is yours. I die."

A little blood bubbled at the purple lips, and he died.

Sir Tremalin turned to look at the thing he had taken from the dead knight's head. It was not steel, it was bone. A long, fine, snouted skull with curving teeth and great round nostrils and eye-holes. The skull of a dragon.

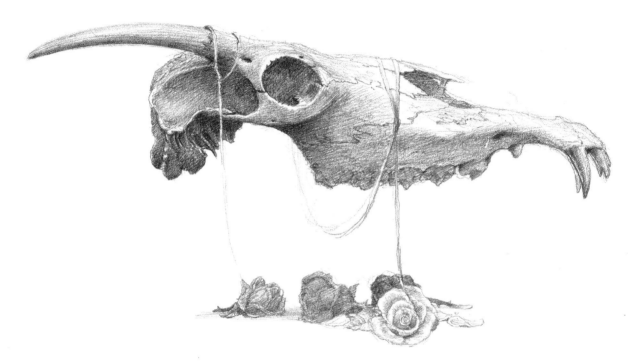

The City of Beausoleil welcomed its deliverer with trumpets and with bells, with cheering and with ribbons and thrown roses. Sir Tremalin rode through the rejoicing streets to his new palace, where choirs sang his praises. Nobody seemed to notice his shifty looks or his battered old armour. He stood on the steps of the palace and waved to the people, but all the time his eyes flickered to and fro, as though he was in wild country full of snares and dangers. He held the dragon helm under his left arm, wrapped in a black cloth he had found in the dead knight's tent. When the cheering was at its loudest he muttered to Dai out of the corner of his mouth.

"See that you know where my horse is stabled."

There was a great feast that night in Sir Tremalin's honour. He sat enthroned on a dais, with Dai at his shoulder to see to his needs (he had insisted on that). He ate and drank from pure gold ware. He was robed in ermine and velvet. The chief men of the city brought him rich gifts. Their daughters smiled at him with sparkling eyes.

Sir Tremalin answered politeness with politeness, smiles with his gap-toothed, lop-sided leer. He spoke little, but ate well and seemed to drink more than well. Only Dai noticed that though his gold goblet went often to his lips it did not seem to become much emptier. And every now and then his hand would wander down to touch the thing that lay beneath the throne, wrapped in black cloth.

When at last the feasting was done and the guests all departed the servants of the palace showed Sir Tremalin to a sumptuous room with a great soft bed, but then he sent them all away and told Dai to sleep across the doorway and make sure no one entered. Before he slept he packed his armour into a bolster-case, padding it with torn sheets so that it should not clink.

An hour before dawn he woke Dai with his finger to his lips. They stole through the sleeping palace. In the banqueting hall they filled another bolster-case with food from last night's feast. Then they found a door and stole round, slipping from shadow to shadow, to the stables, where they loosed Sir Tremalin's horse and the pack-horse. They padded the hooves with sacking and led the horses down to the city gate. A sentry barred their way.

"I am lord of this City," whispered Sir Tremalin. "I must go to the black tent and guard the ford. Open the gate."

The sentry did not seem to think this strange. He opened the gate. They led the horses down and through the swirling water. In the black tent Sir Tremalin armed himself. As the sun rose they rode off between the trees.

They travelled all day. Sir Tremalin hardly spoke, but muttered to himself much as usual. That evening as they sat by the Red Knight's tent he took out the dragon-helm and turned it this way and that, handling it always through the cloth. Twice he lifted it towards his head as if to try its power, but then muttered and wrapped it up and put it away. They slept in the shelter of the tent and travelled on next morning. Still the quick storms came and went.

At noon they came to the black glade with the poisoned well. Sir Tremalin halted at the entrance. He half unwrapped the skull and held it in front of him. The pale bone gleamed. It seemed the only source of light in the dark and ghastly wood.

"The first lord of your city," said Sir Tremalin, "he killed a dragon in this place and threw its body down the well."

"That is the story, my lord."

"But he kept its skull, I think."

"I do not know, my lord."

Sir Tremalin stared at Dai, cold and scowling.

"How much do you and do you not know, boy? Did you know that your last lord was old—so old that for nine years past he had set knights to guard the wells so that he would never need to fight a weaponed man? So old that soon he would have died unvanquished? Did the people of your city know this when they sent you to look for a champion?"

"My lord, I do not understand."

"Do you think, after the life I've led, that I cannot tell a baited trap when I see one? Your lord was doomed to die. Your city needed a new guardian for its ford."

"My lord, our city groaned beneath his rule."

"So you may have thought. What ruling could he do, chained to his task at the ford?"

"But my grandmother dreamed her dream. I am sure of that. She is a simple woman, my lord. Many believe she is not right in her wits, but she tells truth."

Sir Tremalin glared at him, then grunted.

"It may be so," he said. "I will tell you my thoughts. There was a dragon once who laired at this well, and your people worshipped it for a god and gave sacrifices to it. Then there came a brave knight who fought and killed it and threw its body down the well. But he kept the head as a trophy, and seeing it your people accepted him as their lord. After a while he found the power in the dragon's skull and began to wear it. But the dragon's brain still haunted the skull, and it entered the knight's brain and changed him so that he was a noble knight no more, but cruel and dragonish. Thus the dragon was still worshipped in your city, and sacrifices were made to it of all the strangers who came by, and their bodies hung from a tree. For years your people worshipped the dragon, unknowing. But when that knight grew old a new champion was needed, so the dragon sent a dream to someone in the city to tell them to send a messenger to find a knight who would rescue them. Any knight would do, the first who was met, for the dragon would see to it that somehow or other he would succeed. So a new young knight became lord of Beausoleil and held the ford until he too grew old . . ."

"But the Green Knight and the Red Knight, my lord? The spell that held them?"

"A better knight than themselves might have proved too noble. He might have scorned the bait. When the right man came, the dragon would see to it that they were beaten. Their wizard power would fail them, and the spell be broken."

"He helped *you* my lord?"

Sir Tremalin drew himself up.

"He did not need to. Myself, alone, with my own wits, I did it."

He looked down at the skull, poising it this way and that in his hands.

"Not one of those six noble idiots who drove me along this track could have done the same," he said. "Tell me boy, do you think if I went out among them quietly, wearing this skull, I could strike them down one by one before they knew I was there?"

"You could, my lord, but . . ."

"I am very tempted."

" . . . it might rain."

"It might rain. You are no fool, boy. So . . ."

Sir Tremalin slipped from his horse and strode across the glade with the half-wrapped skull beneath his arm. He reached the well and at once, without giving himself time to change his mind, tossed the skull over the coping. There was a rattle and a splash, then silence. He came back more slowly, shaking his head in a dazed fashion, mounted and rode on, muttering as usual, through the songless forest. They slept at the Green Knight's tent.

Next morning, when they were nearing the forest edge, Dai suddenly spoke.

"My lord, I think you have done well."

Sir Tremalin scowled.

"What you think does not matter," he said. "But what will Sir Galavail and those other noble ninnies make of it all? Is it within their understandings? What you must do, boy, is ride ahead and tell them how I have fared. Tell them everything. Say how I won my fights by unknightly means. Spare nothing, only try and get into their heads this one point, that only I, whom they think a false knight and a traitor and a coward, could have fulfilled this quest. Not one of them could have done it, for all his pure heart and shining armour. It was my quest and mine alone. Last of all tell them about the dragon-helm, and how easily I could have used it against them, and chose not to . . . nor was it because of the rain, boy, though that thought tipped the balance—it was because I am not a pure and noble knight. Those who came before me were, or thought they were. They thought their virtue was proof against the power of the dragon. I am no such fool. I tell you again, boy, this was my quest, and only I could have brought it to an end. Those others who went before me had no such luck, and in each of them the dragon lived again, and all was to do again, until one such as I undertook the quest. Tell the six fools that—and tell them too, if you wish, that you think I have done well."

"That was not what I meant, my lord. Listen."

They reined their horses in and waited. Far off to left and right faint noises were beginning, musical twitterings, trills, long and liquid notes. Sir Tremalin frowned.

"What does this mean?" he said.

"The birds are coming back to the forest, my lord."

Sometimes there shivers through his limbs an after-tremor of the Powers he once dealt with. The shudder jerks him awake. Tense. Are they returning, even now? Did the woman make some slip in her closing-spell? Will he never know peace? Slowly he pivots his left fore-arm from where it lies on his chest, twisting the wrist, probing upward with his fingers. Five inches above his face the tips touch stone. They feel for a place. Then enquire. Yes, through all its cold mass the stone lies at peace—so, then, can he. The tension melts from his sinews. There is power in stone, power of silence, power of waiting. It takes power to speak with that power.

Broodingly he remembers the Work . . . the men chanting as they hauled at the trace-thongs . . . the clatter of flint hammers in the quarry . . . the lap of wavelets between the raft-logs . . . the pad of the basket-women, stately under their loads of chalk . . . the deep thud as a hauled stone tipped to the next roller . . . and a single controlling mind hearing all these, guiding each hammer-tap, calming the sea beneath the rafts, pouring strength into the muscles of the men and the spines of the women so that they could each haul or carry their more-than-human load, their share of the Work. Eighty-one stones. Stones of power, that must be fetched out of the earth, shaped in the quarry, floated over the calmed sea, hauled along winding rivers and on up the last long hills, to stand like a dance of giants on the bare upland. A single mind controlling it all. The tribes mindless in the grip of that mind. A man would haul at a trace-thong, shoulder to shoulder with his brother's killer—neither would remember the blood-feud. A woman would carry all day from the ditch to the tip with her three-week child unfed, and the child would not wail. Thirty years' labour poured into a summer. Then the tribes trudging home to their harvests, and the stones silent on the silent upland, filled with their power.

His hand falls back to his chest. Power in stone . . . Peacefully he plays with the knowledge, gives it a shape, a stone life . . . thought slides into dream . . .

ITH his box on his back Sly trudged into the village. A hog-hole he saw at once, a couple of dozen rubbishy little hovels round a church no better than a barn. Lucky to pick up fourpence here, but a man must work his trade and take what he can get, or he'll lose his self-respect, and that's all that matters, isn't it?

One of the hovels was trying to pretend it was an inn. That is to say it had a branch of dead broom lashed to the doorpost. Sly went into the dark little room, put his box down where it would be noticed, bought himself a small mug of cider and a hunk of black bread, and waited for his customers to come in from the fields.

They came. Without seeming to look at them he reckoned them up—four Bumpkins, two Hicks and a Clod. They stared at the stranger, and even longer at his box, which was a three-foot cube, bright-painted with stars and signs, and had air-holes in the top. Occasional scratching noises came from inside it, and once a strange mewing hiss. (Sly had a trick of casting his voice.) He sat relaxed. No need to get into conversation, start up a patter—one of them would ask in a moment, one of the Hicks. Hicks always liked to get their word in . . .

"What've you got in your box, then?"

"Cockatrice," said Sly in a bored voice.

"Cockawhat?" said the Clod.

"Never met a cockatrice?" said Sly. "Well of course you haven't, or you wouldn't be here, in this charming little village of yours. Instead there'd be a fine stone statue of you in the place where you met the cockatrice."

"Give us a look, then," said the Clod, hog-eager.

Sly sighed.

"Don't you listen?" he asked. "You *can't* look at a cockatrice. If you look at him at the same moment he looks at you, and your eyes meet . . ."

He snapped a bony finger and let the sound die in their ears.

". . . you turn to stone," he whispered.

"Gor!" said the Clod.

"Cold, hard stone, never to move again," said Sly.

They thought about it. Sly sensed their slow minds grinding. He made the mewing noise come from the box. The Hick who had first spoken stared at him, then quickly away.

"What's your cockatrice look like then?" he asked the air in front of him. Quite quick, for a Hick, thought Sly.

"Well, he's mostly a sort of brassy colour," he said. "Silver stripes along his back. The front of him's a bantam cock, far as the legs, but all behind there his tail end's more a big lizard. If you were fool enough to look at him once, you'd look at him twice."

"You seen him, then?" asked the Hick, still to the air.

"You could say so," said Sly.

"Why you not turned to stone then?" shouted the Hick.

The Bumpkins and the other Hick banged their table and yelled with triumph at the cleverness of their companion. Even the Clod got it in the end. Sly smiled at the uproar and pulled from his belt-purse a square of polished yellow metal which he breathed on and rubbed on his sleeve. Then he twisted away and held the thing up so that he could see the men's reflection.

"You could say I am seeing you, my friends," he said. "I say I am not. All I am seeing is your image. That is how I know what a cockatrice looks like."

They argued the point among themselves till the next thought struck them.

"Give us a look, then," pleaded a Bumpkin. "Give us a look in your bit of brass."

And they came crowding round, hooked. Sly resisted—the cockatrice was not for show. He was taking it to the Emperor of Tartary, who needed it for the execution of criminals since his religion did not allow him to shed blood. What would happen to the village, to the whole countryside, if it got loose? Why, he took his own life in his hands each time he opened the lid to feed the monster. And so on.

Twenty minutes later he was out in the road with the whole village—Bumpkins, Wenches, Hags, Clods, Besoms, Hicks, the lot—crowding round, each eager to pay their farthing and take their peep in the brass mirror. The mirror, it has to be said, was not very good. The metal was well polished but there was a slight ripple on it which made the reflection waver. Still, if you looked carefully you certainly saw something moving in the depths of the box, with a front end like a bantam and a back end not like any bird that ever was born. All the time the horrible mewing hiss came from the box, and Sly would listen and suddenly snatch the lid and cram it down and say the creature was restless and might try to flap out and then they would all be stone. That added to the excitement.

Half of them had had their peep when Sly sensed a change, a hush at the edge of the crowd. He put the lid on the box and turned, smiling. The crowd parted respectfully, and he saw there was no need to worry. It was only a Dotard, leaning on the shoulder of a Clodling. A dotard of Dotards, snow-white beard, eyes deep under shagged brows—the village priest, no doubt, but a Dotard for all that.

"What is happening?" he quavered.

The whole crowd tried to tell him at once. He came doddering through, leaning on the Clodling's shoulder. Sly started into his patter. The Dotard

listened, nodding and wheezing, and listened again with his head cocked
to one side when the mewing noise came, sudden and loud, from the box.
He groped and found a farthing. The crowd whispered among themselves
as Sly pushed the old fool into place and positioned the mirror.

Sly inched the lid up. Suddenly the Dotard straightened from his crouch.
He had both hands on the rim of the box. For all his age he was stronger
and quicker than Sly had guessed. He wrenched the box away and tipped
it right over.

"Don't look! Don't look!" yelled Sly.

But already most of the village had seen an outraged bantam-cock
running across the mud road. Fastened over its tail-feathers was a leather
extension painted with scales.

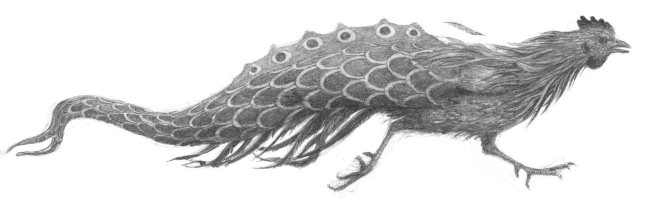

Sitting on a sun-baked rock Sly stared back over the plain. Behind him
bare foothills rose towards mountains. He brooded. There was one particular village in that plain, three days' journey away now, but here at this
moment in his thoughts . . . of course he had been caught out before, jeered
at and pelted before, had his takings seized back before, but for it to happen
there! Clods, Bumpkins, Hicks and a Dotard! If you'd lumped the contents
of their skulls together they wouldn't have added up to one brain . . . He
could get another bantam, make another lizard tail—no need for a new
box, as they'd thrust the old one over his head when they pushed him out
of the village . . . but their jeering! There'd been a note in it, as though
they thought it was Sly who was the Clod . . . something they knew and
he didn't, something about the Dotard . . . Well, one day Sly would come
back and teach them a lesson. A man has to keep his self-respect. That's
all that matters, isn't it?

39

Just below where he sat the sun's heat bounced back from a flat rock. Beyond that the slope dropped away out of sight. He heard a sudden chirruping shriek, a small animal in terror. A mouse raced up on to the rock with a weasel looping behind it. Instead of pouncing at once the weasel overtook the mouse, heading it off and driving it back shrieking over the rock. Sly did not interfere. If the weasel chose to torment its prey before killing it that was none of his business; in fact it fitted his thoughts about Bumpkin village to watch the game played out.

But that did not happen. As the mouse came skittering back on a new line it suddenly froze still. The weasel froze too. Six inches in front of the mouse the surface of the rock had moved, had risen and become a large, squat lizard, the exact colour of the rock. Sluggishly, on splayed legs, it waddled forward and ate the mouse in a single gulp. It raised its head towards the weasel, which arched its back and spat. Out of the lizard's spine rose a bright purple fin. The weasel's brown and white fur turned grey. It did not move again. It was stone.

Still with its tail towards Sly, the lizard lowered the fin and sank down on to the rock. So exactly did its colour match the surface that it seemed to vanish, but with the stone weasel to guide him Sly could just make out where it lay.

He sat still, shaking with terror and thrill, and then nerving himself to move. When he did so it was with a thief's caution. First he undid the hinge-lacings of his box and laid the lid aside. Then he rose and carrying the box bottom up crept down the slope, step by slow step, not daring to dislodge one pebble. All the time he watched the surface of the rock in front of the weasel. His neck-muscles ached with tension, ready to jerk his head aside at the slightest movement. Only as he banged the box down did the lizard stir, and then it was too late.

Sly weighted the box with a boulder and scrambled back for the lid. He slid it probingly under until he felt the lizard scrabble against it. Firmly he slid the box towards him, forcing the lizard up on to the lid, until he had box and lid fitted together. He put his hand under the lid, closed his eyes, and turned the box over, keeping the lid closed tight as he did so. With a sigh of relief he heard the lizard flop first against the side then down on to the bottom. He weighted the lid down and paused, trembling.

The weasel caught his eye and he picked it up. It seemed to have been carved from a dark stone, smooth and very heavy. It was perfect in every hair and claw. He fetched his pack and put it away.

Now he realised that he would need to open the lid in order to replace the lacings. He hesitated. The lizard had made no sound. At last, with his tongue flickering over his lips, he got out his brass mirror and polished it on his sleeve. He knelt by the box and inched the lid up, holding the mirror at the proper angle to show him the bottom. It was dim down there (as it was meant to be, so that Bumpkins should not see too clearly). He made out a dark shape on the wood of the bottom. It did not stir. He opened the lid further to let in more light.

Now the rippled image moved. The fin rose. Large eyes opened, gazing up. In the blurred depths of the brass the two sight-lines met, Sly's and the lizard's. Even like that, even so faintly encountered, Sly felt the icy shaft of the creature's gaze lance into his brain, into his soul.

The neck-muscles knew what to do. They jerked the head aside and he staggered back, letting the lid slap down. It took an hour for the sun to warm him through. He fastened the lacings by touch and made his way down the mountain.

Next morning he had a slice of luck. He met a merchant on the road and sold him the weasel for five silver coins, which meant that he'd have no need to earn his living as a mountebank for a good few days. The idea came to him that he might now be able to give up travelling and settle in a rich town where he could make his living as a dealer in statues. Dogs, cats, squirrels . . . people? Why, yes, if he could find a busy orphanage and make a deal with its warden . . . But before any of that there was the matter of Bumpkin Village.

Deliberately Sly waited till Sunday before he went back.

Everybody was in the little mud church, the people on their knees, the Dotard wheezing through the prayers. Sly waited in the porch for the last Amen.

He flung the door open, strode to the bottom of the aisle and put his box down.

"You wanted to see a real cockatrice," he cried. "Well, I have brought you one!"

Perhaps there was something in his voice that told them that this time he did not lie. They stayed where they stood, all but the Dotard, who came doddering down the aisle, leaning as always on his Clodling's shoulder.

"Well, well," he wheezed, "a cockatrice? A real one? I did not believe that such a thing could be. I would like to see that."

Sly stood back and flung the lid up, keeping his head turned well away. The priest came blundering up, so stupid-eager that he let go of the Clodling and almost blundered into the box. He put a trembling old hand on the edge. What if he turned it over as before? Sly tensed to dart away. He might lose his cockatrice, but he would have a church full of statues. Very striking some of them might be . . . *And* he would have his revenge . . .

The Dotard craned over the box.

"My friend," he murmured, "I think your cockatrice is dead."

Sly took a pace forward, raising his arm to strike the old man in his fury and disappointment. As he did so he glanced down into the box.

The purple fin was raised, the pale eyes staring upwards, meeting Sly's glance. The ghastly shaft seared through brain, soul, body, and he was stone.

"Put the lid back," said the priest. "Do not look, anyone. Be careful."

They did as he said, among whispers and mutters of shock. They waited for his next order. He would know what to do. He had been a scholar, a dweller in cities, adviser to kings, who had come back in old age to the village and people of his birth.

"Not a cockatrice, of course," he said. "There is no such animal—it is a fable. I think our unfortunate friend must have found a basilisk, but let us not grieve too much for him. He might have done greater harm if he had been allowed. Now I have read that there is only one safe method for dealing with a basilisk. Does anyone possess a good mirror?"

It happened that there was a woman who had just such a thing in her hut. Long ago she had been servant to a gentlewoman, who had given the useless luxury to her as a wedding-gift. She ran and brought it. They carried the box out into daylight. The priest made them all stand back while he opened the lid and then held the mirror flat over the box, so that it reflected straight down. He tilted it slightly this way and that, to make sure. Then he borrowed a crook from a shepherd and prodded around in the bottom of the box until he felt the tip scrape on stone. Satisfied, he turned the box over. A stone thing clattered out.

"Why," said someone, "'tis nowt like a cock at all. 'Tis more of a great lizard."

"A dragon, you mean," said someone else.

"Yes, that's what it is," said the Hick who had first spoken to Sly in the inn. He always liked to get his word in.

"'Tis a dragon," he said, "and look, why, you'd only need to put some kind of spear in the fellow's grip where he's got his arm up and he'd do for St Michael, and then we'd have our own holy statue, like we've always wanted, St Michael killing the dragon."

"St George, he was the one with the dragon," said someone else.

The old priest smiled and nodded as they argued it out. They were good simple people. Then he reached out and felt for the shoulder of the boy he needed to lead him everywhere, and told him to take him home for his dinner.

Under the rock there are no seasons. No summer can warm so deep, nor ice-blast chill. But sleeping or waking, he feels in his veins the movement of the circling earth as it hauls the sun from across the equator and sends it south again. The faint invisible rays of the zodiac tingle through his nerves. He wakes one morning and knows the season. The year poised between green summer and grey winter. Day and night equal. The time of the Great Rite.

He remembers a soft dawn wind, a sky of fading stars. Among the mighty stones the priests wait, gazing east. There faint bars of pallor streak the darker blue. The chants begin, voice and answer echoing from the stones and floating out over the upland where, thousand upon thousand, the tribes have gathered for the Rite.

The light grows. The King comes up the stone avenue between the tribes, a young man robed in the yellow and gold of harvest, crowned with a wreath of seeded millet. The tribes moan in the dawn wind. They mourn. Head high, he walks between them.

The Bearer of the Axe, another young man, comes out from among the stones holding the Axe aloft like a battle-standard. It is a strange weapon, a carved haft eight foot long with a heavy bronze head sharpened along one edge and with three up-curved hooks on the other. It is not a battle-weapon, it is the Axe of the Rite.

Louder and louder the moaning wafts on the wind. The King and the Bearer meet at the Outer Stone. The King kneels, bowing his neck. The Bearer waits with the Axe aloft. The chanting priests watch the eastern horizon, where the pale bars have turned bright gold. A shaft of light shoots over the rim of the world. The chant snaps short.

In the silence the Axe falls.

Now the tribes wail. They tear at their clothes, they claw at their cheeks, they pour earth on their heads. Using the loops already knotted into the long hair the Bearer fastens the severed head to the hooks of the Axe and carries it through the chanting priests, holding it high and touching each stone with it as he passes. Four priests climb onto the Outer Stone, carrying a wooden platform on their shoulders, and the new Bearer is lifted to stand on it. When the old Bearer returns he passes the Axe up to his successor, who holds it high so that all the tribes can see. The priests strip the old Bearer naked and robe him in the green of spring. They place a crown of holly on his head. Now he is King, King of the Year.

As the new King passes down the avenue between the tribes they laugh with joy. They cheer each footfall. They hug each other and sing. Behind him, high on the Outer Stone, the Axe blesses his going. Seen from far off it is not a weapon. It shines in the risen sun, a blade of ripe wheat.

. . . so it shines in the man's memory, seen from far off, from across countless years. It floats in his mind's eye as he drifts towards sleep. It changes, it gleams in the light of a holy lamp where it hangs above the bed of a wounded king who can neither live nor die . . . now it is a sword, gleaming over a moonlit lake, till a hand rises from the water to clasp it . . . now it is another sword, hanging in its scabbard beside a throne . . .

T HE Queen put out her arm, caught her stepson Alexander as he passed, and hugged him to her bony side. All the ladies of the court of Lyonesse wore dresses so stiff that they felt like armour, but the Queen, though beautiful, felt bonier than any of them, as though the armour was actually part of her body.

"How is my little Quick-heels to-day?" she said.

The King frowned. He had not heard the nickname before, though everyone else in the court knew it.

"Quick-heels?" he said.

"He is so skilful at avoiding combat with the other boys," said the Queen with her pretty smile. "I think it is very sensible of him. What is the use of taking endless blows on the head? It is not good for the brain."

The King's frown deepened.

"The taking of blows is a test of courage," he said. "We have need of courage in Lyonesse. Come here, Alexander."

He reached out beside him and drew from its scabbard the sword that hung there and laid it across his knees. On the dark blue steel a line of gold letters shone. The King tapped them with his finger. These were the only words he knew how to read.

"What is the message of the sword my son?" he said.

Alexander read the sentence out. He too knew it by heart.

"IF THY HEART FAIL THEE, TRUST NOT IN ME."

"A prince must be braver than the bravest knight," said the King, "or his knights will despise him. This has always been so, but especially now in Lyonesse."

"I know, father," said Alexander.

He did, too. Everyone in the little western kingdom would have understood what the King was talking about, and why his frown was so deep. There had long been a prophecy in Lyonesse that one day a dragon would come, and the land would be dragon-ruled, unless someone braver than the bravest could be found to fight it. Nobody had really believed it would happen, until it did.

Twelve years ago, when Alexander was a baby, his mother had died, and had been buried among the Tombs of the Kings. After a while the King had married again, a bride from the far north, and a fine wedding-feast had been prepared. There was a farmer who was fattening six bullocks for the feast, and in the middle of the night he heard a sudden lowing. He jumped out of bed and ran to his window, whence he saw a great flame down among the cattle-pens. He shouted to his wife, snatched up his club and rushed out. He was never seen again. Only his club was found,

smouldering in the scorched grass between the pens. All six bullocks had also vanished.

That had happened on a full-moon night, and was soon forgotten in the excitements of the wedding, but at the next full moon another six oxen were taken from a different farm, and this time the farmer swore he had seen by moonlight the thing that had taken them, and it had been a dragon. Then people remembered the prophecy. And then each knight of the King's court looked at his sword and wondered in his heart whether he was the one who would prove brave enough.

On full-moon nights (they soon realised that that was when the dragon appeared) the knights rode out and stationed themselves at different parts of the kingdom, ready to do battle. There was a famous fighter called Sir Thingal. If anyone was braver than the bravest, he was. By chance (or was it by chance? Had the dragon somehow heard of Sir Thingal's fame, and decided to show the others its power?) Sir Thingal was the first to meet the monster in combat.

Only his charred boots and saddle were found. The answer seemed to be that even Sir Thingal had not been brave enough.

After that the court of Lyonesse became, as it were, a school of courage. The chief test of courage was to take a blow without flinching, so the knights were always buffeting each other in sport, and the boys, as soon as they could walk, were encouraged to scrap with each other. The boys invented a kind of game which they called Melee, after the sort of jousting in which knights picked sides and fought, all together. The game was simple. They lined up on opposite sides of a courtyard, linked arms, put their heads down and charged. Anybody left standing would then go back and charge again.

Alexander did not enjoy this game. He was small for his age, fine-boned and dark, as his mother had been, while the other boys were big-limbed, blond, broad and ruddy. Alexander used to be sent flying in the first charge, until he learnt a trick of squirming sideways at the moment of impact, slipping through, and perhaps tripping an opponent as he went past. The others thought this was cheating, but they could never work out how he did it, so they called him Quick-heels in revenge.

They said it in whispers first, behind his back. Then they spoke the name to his face. Then, somehow, the Queen heard, and called him Quick-heels in front of the King.

The King tapped the gold letters on the sword.

"I do not believe that you are a coward," he said. "But my belief is not enough. You must show everybody that it is true. I shall give orders that any of my young knights meeting you in the palace is to give you a buffet. You will not wince or flinch or cry out. Above all you will not run away."

"May I dodge?" said Alexander.

"Why should a brave man dodge a blow?"

"I have been watching your knights at sword-play," said Alexander. "They are so slow. They wear thick heavy armour and use the heaviest swords they can wield, and then they stand face to face and take it in turns to smite each other."

"That is the proper way. It is the test of true courage."

"I don't think the dragon knows that," said Alexander. "Your knights expect their enemy to stand its ground and smite and be smitten. They don't learn how to dodge a flame-blast or hit a moving target. Perhaps that's why they haven't managed to deal with the dragon yet."

(The dragon was still in Lyonesse, still taking a few cattle every full moon. Sometimes a knight would ride out and try and find it but if he succeeded then he did not come back. People on the whole had grown used to it and did not speak of it much. Only each year there were fewer and fewer cattle in Lyonesse, and people who could count had begun to reckon the time when all the cattle would be gone and the dragon would start taking children.)

The King smiled.

"You are your mother's son," he said. "I will give orders that my young knights are to clout you if they can."

The knights set about the new game with a will, but soon they found it frustrating. Sometimes one of them would manage to catch Alexander a buffet, which he stood without flinching and then bowed politely to his attacker, though his head was still ringing. But usually the flailing fist struck air, and occasionally the attacker lost his balance and finished up on the floor. This did not make Alexander any more popular in the court, so it was a difficult time for him.

Once a week he used to make his way along the cliff path to the Tombs of the Kings, which was a place of ancient magic where his ancestors had been buried for forty generations. Huge standing stones rose from a gaunt headland that looked out southward over the sea. Here Alexander would put flowers on his mother's grave and kneel and pray for a while, and then make his way back to the castle, which stood on the next headland. Half way along, the path dipped and the cliffs gave way to a broken rubble of rocks which sloped down to a small sandy beach. On either side of the beach tilted ridges of rock ran out into the sea.

One evening as he was passing this place Alexander heard a commotion below, a fierce roaring and a woman's voice screaming for help. There was a full moon rising. It would soon be the dragon-night and he had been anxious to be home, but after staring for a moment he leaped his way down from rock to rock to the beach. He raced across the sand, drawing

his sword as he went. (All the boys of the court wore swords, not to fight with, but to become used to the feel of them, and to manage them without thinking.)

Alexander ran, balancing his way out along a slippery rock-ridge, to a narrow inlet between that ridge and the next. Here he found two strange creatures. Shrinking herself into the highest cranny of the inlet was a girl with bright green hair and a shining fish-tail instead of legs. Further down, struggling to get at her, was a hideous scaly monster. It had a bony lizard head, big crimson eyes with black vertical slits for pupils. Behind the head a long thin neck, and a body that broadened out then thinned away to a flailing serpent tail. It scrabbled at the rocks, trying to heave itself up the inlet with feeble little legs, like a tadpole's, but the ridges came too close to let it through. All the time the sea waves washed in and out over the pair of them, threatening to suck the girl down in the backwash, or float the monster near enough to reach her.

52

Alexander leaped to the inlet's edge and struck down at the monster's shoulder, but the point of his sword glanced uselessly away. The monster swung its head with vicious speed, but Alexander skipped clear of the jagged jaws, then darted in and lunged twice more, without effect. Another wave washed in, driving him back up the ridge. As it sucked back he came darting to the attack.

The monster was ready for him, or thought it was, but instead of striking at it Alexander leaped clear across the inlet, turning as he landed. The head swung round, but he had his sword-point up and lunged as it came, aiming for the eye. This time the point went home. The hilt was almost wrenched from his hand as the head reared up. There was one wailing cry. The monster collapsed, and the next wave sucked it out to sea.

Alexander wiped his blade on seaweed and slid it into the sheath, then turned to the girl. She stared at him with terrified huge eyes, as though he was another monster.

"Madam," he said, speaking in the special language he had been taught for times like this, "it is my great good fortune to have been nigh at hand to succour you in your most need."

"You . . . you'll let me go?" she whispered.

"As for that, madam, you may go at your good pleasure. But first I would fain hear your name, and your nature, and the nature of yon foul creature I have slain."

She stared at him as though she didn't believe him. Another wave came pounding up the inlet. She loosed her grip and let it take her, sweeping out below him, a lithe white-and-silver shape in the glistening foam. He sighed with regret, but then saw that she had not gone right away, but was waving to him from the deeper, calmer water off the point of the rocks. He picked his way down and stood with the waves breaking over his feet while she balanced herself in the swell. She seemed less frightened, and had recovered her wits enough to speak the special language too.

"Sir," she said, "for your succour I give you my good thanks. My name is Melinissa, and I am of the Merfolk, daughter of the King of all these seas. As for the beast you have slain, I take it for a dragonlet. We have heard rumour of a she-dragon that has come to these shores to lay her eggs. Of my foolhardiness I would fain adventure hither to see if the tale were true."

"Certes," said Alexander, "there is a great dragon that despoils our fields and our cattle. I had thought this might be the very monster, for to-night is the dragon-night, when the moon is full and it takes its prey, but this was of too little size. We have heard in Lyonesse no tale of dragon-spawn."

"Nor would you, sir, for they are of the sea. Know you that every year, on a certain night, the she-dragon comes as close as she may dare to the sea's edge, though a dragon full-grown has great dread of water which is the enemy of the fire that is in her. Yet she comes and lays her single egg and buries it in the sand. Then after a season the dragonlet hatches forth and makes all haste down to the waves, for being small it can breathe only water. There for nine years it has its being, but then its nature changes and it puts forth legs and crawls out upon the land, and thereafter it may breathe only air."

"Why, sure," said Alexander, "against yon creature's side I saw legs as it were weak and new grown."

"And so saw I," said the mermaid, "and I take them for a sign that the change had begun, so in scarce three moons there would have been another dragon to despoil your fields. And each year after, yet another."

"This is ill news. I must haste and tell my father."

"Before you go, sir, take from me this gift. If you are in need, set it to your lips and blow, and I or my kin will succour you, as you this day have succoured me."

She gave Alexander a spiral shell with a hole at the point for a mouthpiece, then waved him good-bye and slid beneath the waves.

The King was not sure he believed his son, until Alexander drew from its scabbard the sword he had plunged into the monster's eye, and they both saw that the blade was all pitted and eaten away with strange acids. The weapon was useless, which that morning had been fine sharp steel. The King called for the Queen, whose advice he took on all matters of importance. Alexander showed her the sword and told her what had happened.

She did not doubt him. She was appalled by the story, but after a while she pulled herself together and smiled and praised Alexander for his quickness and courage. So did the King. As he turned to leave the room Alexander felt happier than he had for many days.

Now it happened that on the wall of the room, close by the door, hung a small mirror. It was not a magic mirror, but all mirrors are magical in certain ways. Alexander glanced into this one as he left, and saw the reflection of the Queen standing behind the throne, staring at his back. The look on her face was that of a furious serpent. Her eyes were crimson, their pupils vertical slits.

Next morning Alexander had vanished from the palace, and the King's great sword had been stolen from its place beside the throne.

"He has found the dragon's lair and gone forth to slay it," people said. But when Alexander did not come back that night the whole court went into mourning. Nobody called him Quick-heels now.

At the next full moon all the knights of the court rode out to try and meet the dragon and be revenged for the death of their young prince. None of them thought to stay near the palace. Only one watcher waited hidden in the shadows beneath the tower where the Queen's rooms were. He kept his eyes on her windows, waiting for a great bat-winged shape to glide forth. Nothing happened until an hour before midnight, when he saw a sudden quick gleam at the foot of the tower, as a small door opened on oiled hinges. The door closed and the gleam was gone, but then a human figure strode out of the shadows, wrapped in a long cloak. Whoever it was needed no lantern, so bright was the moon.

The figure walked along the cliff and never looked round—who else would dare be out at the dragon-hour? The watcher followed silently behind.

The figure reached the Tombs of the Kings and vanished among the standing stones. The watcher hurried his pace. For a moment he seemed to have lost his quarry, but then he heard a voice mouthing a strange chant in an unknown language full of hissing sounds. Slipping from shadow to shadow between the stones he came to the central circle where a single huge stone, older than any of the tombs, lay on its side. There he saw the Queen.

She was standing on the central stone with the cowl of her cloak thrown back and her white arms stretched out towards the full moon. The chant became louder and wilder. She paused. With her arms she marked out an invisible circle in the air. She gave a wailing call, the voice of an animal, not a human being. As the call died away the outstretched hands sprouted hooked talons. The ivory arms wrinkled and grew scales. The whole head changed shape, grew a long snout, jagged jaws, unblinking scarlet eyes, humped nostrils from which thin smoke curled up. The cloak fell away as the body exploded into its new shape, an enormous scaly lizard, wingless, but with a fin like a row of rose-thorns running the length of its spine. It raised its snout to the moon, blew out a quick flare of flame and stalked away between the tombs in search of its prey.

Prince Alexander (who was, of course, the watcher) made his way down to the little beach at the foot of the cliff path. There he put to his lips the shell Melinissa had given him and blew. No sound seemed to come, but before he had finished a merman rose out of the waves, driving two dolphins harnessed to the shell of a giant clam. Alexander stepped into the clam and sat down. The merman cried to the dolphins, which drew the shell skimming over the calm sea, round to the sea-cave where Alexander had been hiding. There he found Melinissa and her father the Merking waiting. He told them what he had seen, and together they made their plans.

Next morning when the knights rode in two were missing. Both had had the bad luck to meet and challenge the dragon. Everyone assumed that the same thing had happened to Alexander. Only the Queen insisted that she was sure he was still alive and that everyone must go on searching for him —it was as if it had been her own child she had lost, so eagerly did she ask for news. But no trace of the Prince was found, and the moon waned in the sky and grew big and the next dragon-night came round.

This time there was no watcher beneath the palace wall, but the caped figure strode forth again along the cliff path to the Tombs of the Kings. Again the Queen faced the moon, raised her arms and spoke the dragon-spell. Again she exploded into her true shape.

She raised her head to the moon and breathed her flare. As the flame died Alexander stepped from behind the stone where he had been hiding and stood plain in the moonlight.

"Good evening, stepmother," he said.

For an instant the huge head poised, frozen with astonishment. Then quick as striking snake it swung, and a blast of flame roared from its gullet. But Alexander was no longer where he had been standing. The flame scorched past on either side of the stone which sheltered him, blackening the grass ten paces back. As the dragon drew breath he stepped into the open.

"Then it was your child I slew," he said. "I am not sorry for that."

The dragon lurched at him. Its head and neck were deadly quick, but its big body was clumsy among the stones. He skipped aside and darted away, watching for the instant when the jaws would gape to blast the fire forth. The instant came. The yellow flame caught the corner of his cloak as he whisked into the shelter of another stone. He slipped the cloak from his shoulders and beat the smoulderings out with his palm, then stepped into the open.

"The King my father will hear of his wife's doings on dragon-nights," he said.

She lurched at him again, and again he flicked out of reach. So for a while he played a fearful catch-as-catch-can, in and out among the stones, learning her ways, trying to judge her speed, finding how long a pause she needed before she could summon up another flame-blast. He would show his cloak one side of a stone for her to strike at, then slip away on the other, or step right back and be out of reach as the long neck snaked round the corner to roar its fire at nothing.

But the dragon learnt too. Twice she almost tricked him by holding back part of a flame-blast to roar it at him while he thought she was still having to draw breath. It seemed that she could not do this at all easily and he quickly learnt the signs, but before that he had felt the edge of her flame on his left arm. The sleeve was burnt clean away and the flesh beneath scorched almost to screaming, but he kept his head, and she did not.

For all the time as he darted from stone to stone, or loitered a second in the moonlight, Alexander taunted the dragon. Taunted her with her clumsiness, with her ugliness, with her greed in swallowing whole cattle, with her boniness when she turned herself by magic into a woman, with what the King would do when he found out the truth, and above all with the fact that he, Alexander, Prince of Lyonesse, had slain her child the sea monster. Soon she was reckless with rage, darting and lumbering among the stones, heedless of hurt to herself in her efforts to trap him.

When he saw this Alexander deliberately taunted her round to the area of stones furthest from the palace. There he sheltered from a flame-blast, but instead of stepping out to taunt her as soon as it was over he flitted away between the stones to the start of the cliff path. The dragon was still searching where she had last seen him when he turned and shouted "Now I am going to my father the King!"

He raced down the twisting path.

He did not know how fast she could move in the open, so he had wanted to give himself as much start as he could. It was as well that he had done so. For so large and clumsy-seeming a creature she was desperately quick as soon as she was clear of the hindering stones and could come charging down the path. He would never have reached the palace before she caught him, but that was not his plan.

He heard the thud of her feet and the scrape of her scaly tail closer and closer behind him, but he did not dare look round for fear of missing his footing on the rough path. He came to its lowest point, where the cliffs gave way to tumbled rock. He heard a change in the snort of her breathing as she drew breath for a blast of fire. He darted to the right and flung himself down among the boulders. The flame roared harmlessly above him.

At once he was up and leaping away. The dragon hesitated, eyeing the sea, snaking her head this way and that. Grown dragons are afraid of water, as Melinissa had told him, because they are creatures of fire. But to-night the sea was silky calm under the round moon. It was high tide, and right to the horizon there was not one ripple. She had only to come carefully down, not giving him a chance to dart past her on either side, and she had him trapped. At the bottom there was only the little bay, smooth as the sea, except in one place where someone had been digging.

So she came slowly down over the rocks, not breathing fire, but making certain he could not escape. Alexander backed away before her down to the shore, until he was almost at the sea's edge, with the hummocks of dug sand beside him. He stood there, weaponless, waiting, while the dragon came closer and closer. At each step she paused and eyed the smooth sea. Now she was well in range. She drew back her head and opened her mouth, so that he could see far down the black gullet. The flame spewed. At the last instant Alexander flung himself down into the trench he had dug that dusk.

The dragon, expecting to make an end of it, had breathed her fullest blast and could not see what was happening inside the sheet of fire. The moment it faded Alexander was out of his trench and darting round between her and the cliff. In his hand he held his father's sword, which he had left ready in the trench, and as the head swung to follow him he attacked, darting in and lunging for the eye. At once she whipped her head back out of reach, so he thrust instead at the scaly chest, though the best blade ever forged could not pierce that magical armour.

Still she did not like it and struck at him with her fearsome jaws, but he had the sword ready and twisted aside, lunging two handed for the eye-socket as he did so, forcing the head back out of reach and then dashing in to thrust for a softer place under the foreleg.

It was a hopeless fight. In a few more seconds, despite his pestering, she would have drawn breath for another flame-blast, and this time there was no trench to hide in. But Alexander only needed those few seconds. He had to keep her busy, furious, with all her mind on him and his attacks, so that she did not notice until too late what was happening in the sea behind her.

For there beneath the smooth high tide Melinissa's father had been waiting, the Merking, lord of all those seas, and now he summoned his powers. He harnessed the haul of the big moon. He loosed the energies of ocean. He made a wave.

Behind the dragon's back the dead flat water rose, humped itself, became a ridge, a long dark hill of water rolling towards the shore, faster and faster, foam now glittering along the curled top, leaning high over the glassy black curve beneath, and now, sudden in the silence, crashing in roaring foam over the rock spurs either side of the bay.

Poised for the finishing blast the dragon heard that thunder. She turned her head. She saw the immense and foaming weight of ocean funnelling into the bay. Before she could move three steps the great wave swallowed her.

There were merfolk riding the wave. With strong hands they seized Alexander by the arms and bore him upward through the smother of foam, threshing with silver tails against the rush, back from the tumbled rocks where the wave crashed down, and out in the suck and slither of the backwash. Then as the sea grew calm they set him on his feet in the shallows and he walked wearily up the shore to see what happened to his enemy. His scorched arm, forgotten in the duel, throbbed with pain.

The dragon lay full length at the foot of the rocks where the wave had hurled her, but she was not dead. Indeed she was beginning to struggle to her feet and the whole hideous business might have been all to do again if Alexander had not reached her in time. He drove his sword through the eye-socket deep into the brain.

Then he made his way out to the end of the rocks to thank the Merking for what he had done.

When Alexander's father saw the body of the dragon he at first refused to believe that it could be his Queen, though indeed she had vanished from the palace, no one knew where, except that her cloak had been found at the Tombs of the Kings. But then someone noticed that on the fourth claw of her left front foot something had bitten deep into the scaly flesh, and they looked and saw that it was the ring which the King himself had put there on his wedding day. After that he believed. Then Alexander took him to the sea's edge and introduced him to the Merking. They made a treaty of friendship (more hopeful than most such treaties, since neither was equipped to attack the other) and talked of arrangements for hunting the other eight dragonlets which had hatched from the eggs the Queen had laid.

To celebrate the treaty and the killing of the dragon a feast was held next full moon at the sea's edge, with candles and lanterns bright along the shore, and the merfolk's pale sea lights glimmering out over still water. There were toasts in land-wine and sea-wine, and the mermaids sang beneath the moon.

At the height of the feast the King rose and proclaimed he would now dub Alexander knight, using the very sword with which he had slain the dragon. But when the weapon was brought to him and he tried to draw it from its sheath he found that the whole blade had been eaten away by the acids in the dragon's blood. He called for another sword, and put the useless hilt down, with the sheath beside it, but as he did so something rattled. He tipped the sheath over with his palm beneath it, and out fell a number of small gold objects. Acid does not eat gold, and they were all that was left of the sword-blade, the letters that had been its motto.

The King picked them out one by one and laid them in order, until he had formed the only words he knew how to read.

IF THY HEART FAIL THEE, TRUST NOT IN ME

There is a dream on his way to waking, and for once it stays clear. Lying in the dark beneath the rock he remembers the dream. Childhood, a cliff, climbing, at the top he would touch the sun . . .

Now he remembers the actual cliff, the waking child, himself long ago. Time has looped back and is crossing over close above that exact moment. If he could reach down as the child reached up, their fingers would almost touch. But the child does not stir, does not understand the presence above him. He is lying at the cliff edge, hands under chin, watching the ravens below.

So far down the curving time-track, but still memory can wheel back and become that moment. That boy . . .

The ravens. Something in their flight, a secret, a key—key to a huge truth that lay all around, invisible energies, powers to be met and mastered . . .

The ravens knew. The boy heard it in their harsh calls, saw it in the swoop of their flight. He would need to understand those calls, read the curve of their flight-paths . . .

Where to begin?

There were priests who had secret knowledge, priests of the oak-grove, of the well, of the burial mounds. They learnt their lore in colleges, each generation teaching the next, but that was not what the boy wanted, not secrets already known, if only to the chosen. This master-knowledge was not for teaching. But it was there. He could feel it at this holy moment, an intense, waiting presence. So near. The whole landscape glowing with its power. His soul seeming to swell, seeming to want to burst out of his body, to float like a bubble up into the secret. There, waiting for him . . .

No one could show him the path. He would have to find it for himself.

The path existed—his grandmother's elder brother had taken it. Certain men—one in a tribe, perhaps, once in a generation—heard the summons, knew the yearning. They left huts and wives and cattle to go out onto a mountain or deep into a forest to live alone. Even there they did not live as men might who were forced by chance into solitariness, but sought greater hardship and further suffering. For nights and days they sat naked in the snows or hung themselves from the branches of a winter tree. Then Powers of mountain and forest came to them till they shook with their presence. They raved. But the Powers whispered in their minds, telling them the path . . .

So, now, the boy. Watching the ravens. The choice made.

Memory looses the moment, gliding over the days. It sees the boy going home, speaking to his uncles while his mother wailed in her hut. The uncles killed a sheep and brewed mead and called the tribe to the death-feast. The boy lay in the middle of the feast, wrapped in his grave-cloth. He was carried out of the village and laid on the hillside. Wearing only the grave-cloth, with only the grave-loaf to eat, houseless, nameless, he began his journey.

No one ever again would travel that path so far, suffer so much, come to such power and knowledge. He had won honour beyond kings, but that was nothing. To walk one step along the path was worth more than all the honour in the world. There were some who did walk only that one step, who barely began to touch the great secret. Suppose the boy had been one of them . . .

The thought causes him to smile. Still smiling he drifts back through dream.

HERMIT

(A Wayside inn where a fisherman and a priest, childhood
friends, have met after many years.)

YOU got our letter?
          Sure.
                    Why do you smile?
Too learned are you now for the crude style
Of fishing folk?
               No. When I was in Rome
I longed for nothing more than news from home.
But . . .
      But?
             Who wrote it for you, may I ask?
None of you read or write. Who did the task?
Our hermit wrote it.
             Hermit?
                   Since you left.
Turned up one March and settled in the cleft
Of Whalehead Cliff. Jack found him in that nook
Kneeling in prayer, with an enormous book
Spread out in front of him. Jack asked a blessing.
And then . . .
        One moment—let me do some guessing.
The hermit begged and got a scrap of fish.
Then, soon (and he would hardly have to wish,
You being generous folk) he was well set—
Clothes for his back, a roof against the wet,
Coals for his winter fire, rugs for his bed,
And every day fresh fish, salads and bread,
With not one penny paid.
             He paid in prayers.
I'll bet he did—boomed out with solemn airs,
Mouthfuls of what you thought was Latin, yes?
Latin's the language if you want to bless.
It is indeed. But that was no more Latin
Than rainwater is wine or sacking's satin.
I know the type—his nose in his great book
Whenever anybody chanced to look . . .
Yes, but . . .
        One moment, let me guess again.
One day a pleasant thought crossed someone's brain,
To wit, a man who reads must also be

66

Able to write—let's ask our saint if he
Will pen a letter for us to young Paul,
So far away, so long away from all
He knew and loved in childhood. Off you went
To Whalehead Cliff and found the hermit bent
Over his book. You asked . . . And he demurred!
How did you know?
                    He could not read a word,
Nor write one either.
                    But . . .
                                Yes, in the end
You begged so strongly he sat down and penned
A letter for you.
                There! Yourself have said it!
The hermit wrote our letter and you read it!
I got your letter and was very glad.
It came from home and it was all I had.
For five long years, until it fell apart,
I kept that parchment nearest to my heart.
During dull lectures I would sneak it forth
And sniff at it and think I smelled the North,
Our North, our gull-ruled, herring-swarming sea . . .
But as for reading it, that could not be.
Not the most learned clerk that ever was
Could read a single word of it, because
There wasn't one word in it!
                            None at all?
Lines, blobs, curls—scribbles such as babies scrawl,
Trying to draw.
                But . . . but . . . but you wrote too . . .
Of course I wrote back. What else could I do?
There wasn't much to write you'd understand.
Rome is so different, so grimy-grand,
And almost every man a priest or monk—
Full of pure thoughts, no doubt, but how they stunk!
I did the best I could with news like that . . .
That's what your letter said?
                                Why, yes . . . My hat!
Of course! You took it up to Whalehead Cliff
For *him* to read! That must have scared him stiff,
Thinking that now you're sure to find him out!
What did he do? Brazened it through, no doubt,

With fancied news from Rome, with his own quaint
Imaginings of cardinal and saint
And angels on the roof-tops, all aglow!
Such miracles he said I'd witnessed, no?
No.
   Not one miracle?
      Well . . . maybe one.
Which was?
    He held your letter to the sun,
Conning it slowly through, drew breath, then read
Unhesitating. This is what he said:
"From Paul, your friend, in Rome. Beware! Beware!
"This morning as we walked in Peter's Square
"The Pope spoke to me of a dream he'd dreamed
"Only last night, a dream in which he seemed
"To stand on Whalehead Cliff, and thence he saw
"The Northmen's long ships driving to the shore,
"The Northmen streaming up with shield and spear,
"Your houses all aflame. This he saw clear
"And certain as if he'd been standing there.
"And then an angel whispered in his ear
"That I must write and warn you, and must say
"The Northmen's ships will beach the very day
"You hear this letter read."
      And that was all?
It was enough! We gathered up such small
Treasures as we could carry, and then fled.
I'll guess again. The hermit stayed.
       He said
A martyr's crown awaited him that day,
But we must go.
    I'll bet he did. That way
He could thieve through your houses, room by room,
While all of you were running from the doom
You thought I had foretold. Me, meet the Pope
Walking before St Peter's! What a hope!
And so, while you were haring down the road
And glancing back over your shoulder-load
For the first sign, the smoke that proves the flame . . .
Why do you smile like that?
      The Northmen came.

Thunder? Drums? The beat of his own slow blood?

No, none of those—horse hooves—five wild ponies, riderless, cantering by. No wonder he woke at the sound. There had always been horses . . .

. . . readying for war, twin-yoked to the chariots, neighing, froth on mane and neck, feeling in their horse-minds the war-lust of the fighters, spear-flinger, whip-wielder . . .

. . . the grove of Epo, tended only by women, pale mares under the rowans, for a man to touch them death by slow drowning . . .

. . . a whole tribe gathered on a hillside to honour their god with a great image which will be seen from all across the plain. But how shall they make it, where shall they dig, standing so close on the curving slope, when the lines they dig must show a watcher far away a great white horse galloping over the green turf? Therefore they have sent for a man, a stranger with strange gifts. He gropes on the hill as though he were blind, for his mind is far off, watching. With his staff he prods out a line. Their mattocks bite down through turf to the clean white chalk. Hovering far off the mind sees the holy horse begin to appear. He holds the horse in his mind . . .

It is there again now as that same mind sinks towards darkness. It glimmers into the forest of his dream, cantering under the trees, moon-white, sacred, tameable only by women . . .

HIANNON was an orphan and lived with her grandmother in a village at the edge of the forest. She was one of Sir Brangwyn's orphans, as they called them in those parts— that is to say her parents were alive but her father was imprisoned in the dungeons of Castle Grim and her mother worked in the castle kitchens to earn money to pay for his food. He had done nothing wrong, but Sir Brangwyn had accused him of stealing deer. Sir Brangwyn liked to have the best men from all the villages in his dungeons, so that the other villagers would stay quiet and good, and hardly dare murmur when he taxed them of every farthing they had. Everyone knew that Rhiannon's father was innocent. If he had really been stealing deer Sir Brangwyn would have hanged him from the nearest tree.

Rhiannon was not allowed to go with her parents to the castle. Sir Brangwyn made a point of leaving the children behind, to remind the other villagers to be good. So she stayed in the village and did her share of the work. Everybody in the village had to work or starve, and since Rhiannon was only nine her job was to hunt in the forest for truffles.

The forest was enormous—nobody knew how big, or what lay deep inside it. Some said that strange beasts laired there, dragons and unicorns and basilisks, which could turn you to stone by looking at you. Others said all that had happened in the old days, and the strange beasts were gone, so now there were only ordinary animals such as boars and deer and wolves and bears. Sometimes Sir Brangwyn would come and hunt these. Hunting was the one thing he cared about in all the world.

Rhiannon never went deep into the forest. She always stayed where she could see the edge. Truffles are hard to find. They are a leathery black fungus which grows underground on the roots of certain trees, and for those who like rich food (as Sir Brangwyn did) they add a particularly delicious taste and smell. Rhiannon always hoped that one day she would find so many truffles that Sir Brangwyn would send her parents home as a reward, but it did not happen. She seldom found more than a few, and sometimes she would dig in forty places and find none.

Exactly a year after the soldiers had come to take her father away Rhiannon went off to the forest as usual. But not at all as usual, she was followed back that evening by a small white horse, no more than a foal, pure silvery white with a silky mane and tail.

The villagers were amazed.

"It must have escaped from some lord's stable," they said, and they tried to catch it, thinking there would be a reward. But before they came anywhere near, away it darted, glimmering across the meadows and into the dark woods. Then they found, to their further amazement, that Rhiannon's basket was full of truffles.

"My little horse showed me where to dig," she said.

This seemed very good news. Sir Brangwyn's tax-clerk would be coming to the village in a few days' time. Truffles were rare and expensive. Perhaps they could pay all their taxes in truffles, and that would mean they would have a little food to spare for themselves this year. So next morning a dozen men and women went up with Rhiannon to the forest, hoping the little horse would come and show them where to dig. But they saw no sign of it and they found nothing for themselves, so at noon they went back to their own tasks, leaving Rhiannon behind. Again that evening the white horse came glimmering behind her almost to the edge of the village, then dashed away. And again Rhiannon's basket was full of truffles.

73

So it went on every day until the tax-clerk came, and the headman brought him a whole sackload of truffles to pay the taxes. This clerk was a monk, who could read and write. He knew things which ordinary people do not know. When he asked how it happened that the village had so many truffles to send, the headman told him. The headman was a simple fellow. (Sir Brangwyn saw to it that the clever ones were in his dungeons.)

That evening the clerk sent for a huntsman and told him what he wanted, and next night the huntsman came back and told what he had seen. He had followed Rhiannon up to the forest, taking care to keep out of sight, and at the forest edge a little white horse had come cavorting out and kissed Rhiannon on the forehead, and then she had followed it in under the trees where it had run to and fro, sniffling and snuffling like a dog, and every now and then it would stop and paw with its hoof on the ground, and Rhiannon would dig there and find truffles. The horse was obviously extremely shy of anyone but Rhiannon and kept looking nervously around, so the huntsman had not been able to come close, but then, when Rhiannon's basket was full, she had sat down with her back against a tree and the horse had knelt by her side and put its head in her lap and gazed into her eyes and she had sung to it. The little horse had been so entranced that it seemed to forget all danger, and the huntsman had been able to creep close enough to see it well.

"And sure, it's a very fine wee beast, your honour," he said to the clerk. "What it'll be doing in these woods I can't be guessing. And it's never seen bit nor bridle, I'll be bound, never seen stall nor stable. As for the colour of its coat, it is whiter than snow, not a touch nor fleck of grey nor of yellow in it. Only one thing . . ."

"Yes?" whispered the clerk, as though he knew what was coming.

"The pity of it is the animal's face, for it's mis-shapen. It has this lump, or growth as it might be, big as my bent thumb between the eyes."

"Ah," said the clerk.

Next morning he left his tax-gathering and hurried to Castle Grim to tell Sir Brangwyn there was a unicorn in the woods.

The great hall of Castle Grim was hung with the trophies of Sir Brangwyn's hunting. Deer and hare, boar and badger, wolf and fox, heron and dove, he had ridden it down or dug it up or hawked it out of the air. But he had never hunted unicorn. Before the clerk had finished his message Sir Brangwyn was on his feet and bellowing for his huntsmen and his grooms, and in an hour he was on the road with a dozen expert trackers and twenty couple of hounds.

The people of Rhiannon's village were glad to see him come. Sometimes when a village had shown him good sport he had let the people off their taxes for a whole year. So here they were eager to help. They beat the woods, they dug traps where they were told, they set watch, but it was all no use. Sir Brangwyn's clever hounds bayed to and fro and found nothing. His trackers found the prints of an unshod foal all over the truffle-grounds, but lost the trail among the trees.

After three days of this Sir Brangwyn's temper soured, and the villagers began to be anxious. Then the tax-clerk explained what Sir Brangwyn had been too impatient to hear before, that the only way to hunt a unicorn is to send a maiden alone into the woods, and the unicorn will come to her and lay its head in her lap and be so enraptured by her singing that he will not see the huntsmen coming.

Sir Brangwyn had not brought any maidens with him, but the village headman told him about Rhiannon. All that night the villagers toiled by torch-light, cutting brushwood and building a great bank of it by the truffle-grounds, high enough to hide a mounted man. In the morning they took Rhiannon up to the forest. When they told her what she had to do she tried to say no, but by this time Sir Brangwyn had learnt where her parents were, and he explained to her what would happen to them if she refused. So she went into the forest and sat down, weeping, in her usual place, while Sir Brangwyn waited hidden behind the bank of brushwood.

For a long while everything was still.

Then, suddenly, there was a glimmering deep in the dark wood and the unicorn came delicately out, looking this way and that, hesitating, sniffing the wind. When it was sure all was safe it cavorted up to Rhiannon and kissed her on the forehead and knelt by her side with its head on her lap, gazing up into her eyes, puzzled why she did not sing. Sir Brangwyn broke from his hide, spurring the sides of his horse till the blood runnelled. The nearing hooves drubbed like thunder.

Then Rhiannon could bear it no more. She jumped to her feet with her arms round the unicorn's neck, dragging it up, and turned its head so that it could see Sir Brangwyn coming.

At once it reared away, giving Rhiannon no time to loose her hold. The movement twitched her sideways and up so that she was lying along the unicorn's back with her arms round its neck and the unicorn was darting away under the trees with Sir Brangwyn hallooing behind, his spear poised for the kill.

The hoofbeats dwindled into the forest, into silence. Then huntsmen and villagers, waiting out of sight beyond the forest, heard a voice like the snarl of trumpets, a man's shout and a crash. Then silence once more.

The trackers followed the hoofprints deep into the dark wood. They found Sir Brangwyn's body under an oak tree, pierced through from side to side. His horse they caught wandering close by.

Rhiannon came out of the forest at sunset. What had she seen and heard? What fiery eye, what silvery mane? What challenge and what charge? She would not say.

Only when her mother and father came home, set free by Sir Brangwyn's heir, she told them something. They had taken her to her bed and were standing looking down at her, full of their happiness in being all three together again, and home, when she whispered four words.

"Unicorns have parents too."

Gently—no storms now, never again—he floats from the inward dark to the dark around him. What has woken him? The echo of the sound dwindles in his drowsy mind, a screech, loud enough to pierce the yards of rock that shield him. Fox? Seagull? Raven? No, he would have slept on. It must have been a human cry, the voice of rage, the screech of a woman railing at a man. What had he done? Some life-blighting cruelty? Some quick little stupidity? Either will be forgotten, buried in the silt of years. But the cry will remain.

He remembers a broad-beamed hut, a king carousing among his fighters, the litter of their feast scattered on table and floor—king, fighters and servants all too drunk to notice the woman slip in through the doorway. Crouched low she scurries between the sleeping hounds to the centre-post. A servant sees her and grunts a warning—too late. She has thrown her arms round the sacred post. Now no one may touch her. She hauls herself upright and begins the cry.

What is the wrong done? A pig stolen? A son ambushed and killed in a blood-feud? Her millet-patch browsed by a neighbour's donkey? There is no knowing, for she is incoherent with rage and grief and her hearers too drunk to unravel the tale, but it does not matter. She has laid hold of the sacred post and called to the King for vengeance. So now his honour is at stake. He houses and feeds his fighters to guard that honour.

Blearily the King peers round the circle of crimson faces. All try to miss his eye—the feast is not over, and there is little glory to be won in a squabble like this. The head will barely be worth carrying home.

The King smiles maliciously and hiccups a name. The fighter rises and gropes his way out, with the woman still babbling her wrongs close behind him . . .

Now the pool of memory wrinkles as he slides back into sleep. The hut, the woman, the fighter, the king—their images quiver and change, becoming the shape of dream—a white-walled, turreted city, with a river running close by. A rich stone hall, glittering with banners, lit with a hundred torches . . . out in the forest, beyond river and meadows, a woman riding a white pony . . . in the hall a hundred knights, brilliant in velvet and silk . . . at their centre the High King, waiting . . .

THE King's custom was this: on a Feast Day he would not sit down to his meal until he had seen some marvel—a mailed knight striding into the hall with his severed head beneath his arm, and the head then speaking its challenge; or a lady riding a white stag and pursued by black hell-hounds; or letters of fire appearing over an empty chair and telling what knight must sit there and what doom would then befall him. Then the King would send the named knight, or choose one if no knight was named, to follow the adventure through, and with luck he would be back by the next Feast Day to amuse the court with his story.

Feast Days went by. Marvels became less wonderful, adventures much like the adventures before, and stories (the hearers began to hint) less true, until one Pentecost it seemed that nothing was going to happen at all and either the custom would cease or the court would go hungry. Hour after hour went by. The steaming meats grew cold. The Queen yawned—and not only the Queen. The knights showed their jealousies in open bickering. Still nothing happened. It was the middle of the afternoon when the King's Chamberlain imagined he heard a slightly different sort of commotion at the far end of the hall and bellowed to the court to stand aside so that the King and Queen could see the cause of it, but it turned out to be only a pretty white greyhound bitch running about among the courtiers.

There were sighs of frustration, groans of hunger. The dog used the space that had opened to move more freely, peering up into the faces of each knight in turn. Though this could hardly be called a marvel it helped pass the time, so the Chamberlain called to the knights, to form a circle and let the dog see them properly. The King, who liked to remind people he too had once been a knight and had adventures, rose and joined the circle.

The dog accepted the arrangement at once. It paced solemnly along, gazing at the faces with a bright intelligent stare. The whisper went round that it must be some lady's pet, come to look for her lover, which gave the wits a chance to make scandalous suggestions as it passed each famous fighter, but it gave no sign that it recognised any of them. It paused slightly longer in front of the King, and there was a hush of shocked amusement, but it passed him by too. It had almost reached the end of the circle when it gave one knight a longer stare, then stalked forward, took the corner of his cloak in its teeth and pulled him into the ring.

Everyone cheered and jeered. The knight blushed scarlet. He was very young, a big-boned, dark-haired lad who had only recently come to court and had already had to put up with a good deal of mockery for his country manners and his earnestness about the ideals of knighthood. The King did

81

not know his name, even. Nor did the Chamberlain, who scurried to find out.

It looked as though the amusement was over, but as the King went back to his seat the dog followed him, tugging the young knight with her. The King sat down, saw what was happening and beckoned. The knight came shyly forward with the dog pacing beside him, still nipping the corner of his cloak in her teeth. The Chamberlain came back just in time to whisper the name in the King's ear.

"It seems, Sir Hugh, that you have been summoned on a quest," said the King. "A small marvel, but it must serve for hungry men."

The court shouted with relief and crowded to the tables. The sound of their feasting echoed among the ramparts as Sir Hugh, now armed in steel from head to foot, rode over the drawbridge with the greyhound trotting ahead to show the way.

The road led through farmland into a forest. A mile in under the trees the greyhound turned along a narrow path and soon after that branched off along no track at all. Hugh had to dismount and lead his horse. The dog darted ahead, but before he lost sight of it it stopped and glanced back to make sure he was still following. Then it vanished. He hurried his pace and pushed his way through undergrowth into an open glade.

The greyhound was on the far side, licking the face of a woman who lay in the shadow of a large tree. A white pony was tethered to one of the branches. The woman was in little danger from beast or outlaw, because a huge dark hound lay beside her, but leapt up at the clank of Hugh's armour, raging and straining at its chain. When the woman rose Hugh saw that she too was chained by the neck to the tree.

This was very much the sort of adventure a knight embarking on a quest might hope to find, so Hugh drew his sword to defend himself from the hound and strode eagerly across the glade, but before he reached the tree the woman had freed herself by simply undoing the collar round her neck. She then quieted the big dog with a word and a pat and whistled to the greyhound, which seemed to have decided it had finished its errand and could now go nosing for rabbits. It came obediently back and let the woman fasten round its neck the collar she had been wearing. At last she turned and faced Hugh.

He had always somehow assumed that any damsel he might be called upon to succour would be pale, lissom, helpless and beautiful. This woman —or girl, rather, not much more than sixteen—was none of those, but a perfectly ordinary girl, sturdy, freckled, with green eyes wide-set in a square face. You would not have looked at her twice apart from her hair, which was certainly remarkable, a vivid orange-red, long, thick and glossy with animal energy. As her eyes met Hugh's she blushed but her glance did not waver. Her chin went up and she gazed at him with a look of challenge.

"Madam," he said, "what would you of me, for my sword and my arm are yours and your enemy is mine?"

"I dinna talk sic speech," she said. "But you'll be hungered?"

"Why, yes, but . . ."

She turned abruptly away and opened a saddle-bag which lay against the foot of the tree. From it she took a flask, a loaf, and pieces of meat. Hugh was taken aback by her brusqueness and ignorance of the formalities, but he was indeed hungry, so he sat down gladly enough and ate. The meat was very tough, hare roasted over flame. The big dog watched him as he gnawed, and growled deep in its throat, but the greyhound paid him no attention, fawning on the girl for scraps. The girl was obviously hungry too, and gnawed away like a man. She made no attempt to talk.

"That is a clever bitch, madam," said Hugh, trying to start a conversation.

"Whiles she's clever, whiles not," said the girl, smiling for the first time —an odd expression, gone in an instant.

"What is her name?" said Hugh, trying again.

"Lady. The dog is Boy. You'll be Hugh, I'm thinking."

"Sir Hugh de la Motte—your champion, madam, if you choose to have me. How did you know my name?"

Again that momentary smile. A pause. An obvious summoning of the will.

"I want you to fight a warlock for me," she blurted.

This was bad news. Hugh's father had trained him to fight other knights, and said that he was good enough to go to the King's court. He had given him advice on how to attempt to deal with such enemies as giants and dragons. At least with those you knew what you might be fighting. Warlocks were another matter.

"In what docs his power lie?" said Hugh, trying not to sound too cautious.

"He takes on the body of a muckle wolf and scours my lands. He kills sheep and cattle. He breaks open the doors of the crofts and takes the bairns from their cradles."

"Can he not be hunted down?"

"He wilna let a dog live in all my lands. He has killed even the dogs that baited my father's bear."

"What can I do? I know something of venery, but no more than other men. I have never hunted wolf."

"There is a thing you can do, Sir Hugh. When we ken each the other better I will tell you."

She turned her head away and scratched behind Lady's ears, clearly determined to say no more. Hugh watched her, thoroughly dismayed. This was not at all what he had expected of a quest, but he had no wish to slink back to court and explain that he had backed out. And the girl herself, despite her strangeness—her lack of manners, her secretiveness, her unnerving smile, her foreign sounding English with its lilt and its odd words—despite all that there was something arrogantly direct and honest about her. He found it difficult to think that she might be trying to cheat or trick him.

"Vouchsafe me, then, madam, to assure me of but one matter," he said. "That this venture you ask of me is such as a man might dare undertake without shame or dishonour either to his own person or the noble order of knighthood."

The green eyes met his. She sighed but did not look away.

"For shame and honour I dinna ken," she said. "But this I ken weel—there is as muckle danger in it as in any fight all the king's knights have ever fought. And if when I tell you my plan you say you dinna like it, I will not call you coward."

"Very well. For your sake, madam, I will attempt the adventure . . . I suppose at least you can tell me your name."

She laughed openly for the first time, and tossed her astonishing hair.

"In the language of my people my name is Cu-fionna," she said. "But for the English I call myself Cynella."

They picked their way back to the road and travelled north till evening, sleeping at a woodman's cottage and riding on as soon as the sun was up. Most of the land was forest. Around mid-day another knight came down the track towards them, wearing black armour and riding a big black charger. Without waiting for the courtesy of a formal challenge the stranger pulled his visor down, lowered his spear and came thundering forward.

Hugh would probably have fought him anyway. It was normal when two knights met, even if they were friends, for them at least to break lances with each other. But this was clearly a rogue knight. Hugh, taken by surprise, had hardly got ready and begun his own charge when the black knight was almost on him. He would certainly have been unhorsed, but just as his adversary crouched to take the impact the greyhound came skimming forward and leaped yelping at the black charger's face.

The charger tried to toss its head aside. The knight, all his attention on Hugh, was not prepared for the movement, so his spear-point wavered and missed. But Hugh, travelling more slowly, had time to adjust his aim. His spear caught the shoulder of the shield-arm where the shield had dropped in the knight's struggle to manage the reins, so it was the knight's own impetus that unhorsed him. He fell with a clang and lay still.

Hugh's next move was supposed to be to dismount, wait for the knight to rise, and then start a sword-fight and hope to teach him a lesson for his treacherous attack, but when he wheeled his horse round and trotted back for Cynella to hold the reins while he fought, he was astonished to see that she had dismounted and had then somehow got her pony's reins tied round her wrist. She was gnawing at them with her teeth.

"Mount, mount!" he yelled. "This is some villain knight! You must be ready to flee!"

She stared at him with blank, bewildered eyes, but then the greyhound came prancing back and leapt up to lick her face. She hugged the animal to her for a moment before pushing it away.

Suddenly she seemed to understand the danger and swung herself into her saddle, but instead of waiting for Hugh to hand her his reins she immediately seized his horse's bridle, shook her own reins and began to hustle both horses along the path.

"Hold hard," said Hugh. "Let me dismount."

"No! Quick! He's waking! Catch his horse as we gang past."

The black knight gave a groan and pushed himself onto his elbow. Cynella ignored him, steering her pony along the edge of the road and dragging Hugh after her. She whistled to the dogs to follow. The black charger was standing broadside on to the track, waiting for its master to rise, as it had been trained to.

"Get him, Boy!" called Cynella.

The big hound leapt snarling forward. The charger reared away and galloped off along the road with Boy snapping at its hocks. Cynella kicked her pony to a canter, still dragging Hugh's horse with her. He shouted to her again to stop, but she shook her head and rode on, leaning forward over the pony's neck, urging it into flight. In the end he had to reach right forward himself and prize her fingers from the bridle before she consented to stop.

But then they were a hundred yards along the track. Hugh looked back. The black knight was trudging after them, waving his sword and bellowing at Hugh for a coward. Hugh started to turn his horse, but Cynella backed her pony and faced him.

"Dinna fight him," she said.

"It is my first true fight."

"And but for . . . but for Lady it would have been your last. Dinna fight him, Sir Hugh. *He* is not my enemy. You gave me your promise, it was *my* enemy you would fight. Any of the braw knights in the court can settle with this fellow, but you're the only one can help me. And I've come so far to fetch you. I canna lose you now. You are no coward. Dinna fight him. Please."

Hugh hesitated. It was not the arguments, it was the plea itself that made up his mind, the effort it needed for her to bring herself to ask. But he was far from happy. He looked at her as the bellowing knight came nearer. For some reason, he noticed, she was wearing the greyhound's collar.

"Very well," he said, then turned his horse and rode on, frowning. Half a mile down the road they found Boy lying panting in the shade. The black charger had vanished. Cynella dismounted to pat the dog and then whistled to Lady, who had been following them, strangely listless. She undid the collar from her neck and fastened it round the greyhound's, who at once perked up. Watching the whole episode through narrowed eyes Hugh had seen that along the inside of the collar there ran what looked at first glance like a pattern of red on the black leather. But he had time to decide that it was more than a pattern, it was writing. He felt a shiver of chill across his shoulder-blades and drew his horse to the far side of the track. Cynella looked up.

"What's with you?" she asked.

"Madam, I think there is witchcraft in that collar."

She nodded.

"I do not meddle in such things," he said.

She came round her pony and put her hand on his mailed knee, looking up into his eyes.

"I'll show you this evening," she said. "I'll tell you the whole tale of it. Gang along with me that far. I'll free you from all promises and you can choose. If I maun find me another champion I will, but I ken weel I canna find a better one."

This time Hugh did not hesitate. He was wholly convinced of her honesty, of the fairness of her offer. Besides that, he was inquisitive. He wanted to hear her story—at least, suppose he did cry off, it would give him something to amuse the court with.

As they rode on she made Hugh talk about himself. Hitherto she had spoken very little, neither asking questions nor answering them if she could help it. Now it was as though she too was needing to decide, and to know as much as she could about him before she did so. So he told her about his home, more of a moated farm than a castle and crowded with his brothers and sisters; of how he, being second son, would need to find his own fortune, so had learnt endless lessons in the arts of knighthood from his lame father, all fitted in between stints of ploughing and haymaking; of his journey to court, and his growing unhappiness at finding it a place of jealousy, idleness and intrigue. She told him nothing in return, but was more relaxed than she had so far shown herself, laughing and sympathising as he talked. He found himself liking her, and admiring her too. She rode her pony as though she and it were one creature. Her dogs adored her.

Towards evening, in a very lonely part of the forest, she left the track and led the way up a stream-bed to a place where a huge old tree had fallen, leaving a small clearing beside the water. The trunk lay along a bank of ground which curved inward, making a natural shelter.

"I found the place ganging south," she said.

"Were you not afraid? There are wild beasts. And wild men."

"I'm safer with Boy than I'd be in a strange house."

"A house would give us a meal. There's no meat left."

She answered with her sidelong glance and smile but said nothing. They loosed the horses to forage the scant woodland grass, then made camp. Cynella whistled Lady to her and undid her collar. She fastened a chain to it and tied the other end to a branch. Then she buckled the collar round her own neck, swallowed and drew a deep breath.

"I'll find supper," she blurted. "You fetch wood and make us a fire."

Hugh stared. His heart hammered. Cynella put her hand on Lady's neck and bent towards her. Lady stood still, obviously quite used to what was going to happen. Cynella hesitated.

"I havena done it afore with a body watching," she whispered. "No. Look. You maun see for yourself."

She put her face close against Lady's and licked the dog's nose several times.

Nothing seemed to change. Lady backed away, turning on Hugh the bright, clever gaze she had worn when she ran among the knights, shook her pelt as though she had just come out of the stream, and slipped away among the trees. Cynella yawned and lay down on the bare ground. Her face was dull, her eyes mindless. She scratched behind her ear with her left hand, wriggled for comfort and fell asleep.

Hugh was breaking up dry twigs when Lady came back with the first rabbit. He had the fire lit by the time she brought the second, which she laid in front of Boy. He seemed quite used to the process and licked her ears in thanks. Then she was off into the woods again, and this time was longer away. Hugh had his rabbit skinned and roasting before she came back with another. She put it on the ground, trotted over to where Cynella lay and licked her face. Cynella sat up, stretched, took the collar off and put it round Lady's neck. Lady ran at once to her rabbit and started to tug and gnaw. Boy was by now snapping the last bones.

Cynella came over and knelt by the fire in silence, watching Hugh turn the rabbit on the spit he had cut. He looked across at her. It was dusk now, and the shadows on her face flickered to the twitch of the flames, but even in that weird light she seemed the same as she had when they first met, proud, shy, direct, vehement, and not any kind of witch. She must have guessed his thought.

"Now you've seen," she said. "That is the one magic I own."

"It is very marvellous."

"I am weel worn to it . . . Och, yon rabbit smells fine, but if you kent how it smells to a dog!"

88

She wrinkled her nose, dragging the odours in. They both laughed.

"That was good hunting," said Hugh. "Three kills in so short a time—must I thank you or Lady?"

"Both of us. My brain, her quickness. That is . . . that is what makes my uncle so terrible."

"Your uncle?"

"He is the wolf you maun fight. When we've eaten, I'll tell you."

"The giftie runs in our kinder . . ."

Cynella paused and glanced at Hugh with a faint mischievous smile.

"Och," she said. "I maun try to talk southron, so you ken weel what I'm saying."

He nodded. It turned out that in fact she could speak almost normal English, but had deliberately chosen not to, as if to insist from the very first on her difference, her apartness from his world. She was full of such distrusts, and he soon learnt why.

"It runs in our family, like the colour of our hair," she said. "You must have the gift, but you must know the secret too. The chieftain of our clan tells the secret to his eldest son, and he passes it on. My father learnt it from his father, but he had no son, so he told his younger brother instead.

"One day my father was out hawking on the moors when he was separated from his friends. A huge wolf came at him silently from behind in broad daylight and took him by the leg and pulled him out of the saddle. It would have killed him, but his spaniel, Hero, attacked the wolf and gave my father a chance to defend himself, and his friends heard his shouts and Hero's barking and came galloping up and drove the wolf off. But by that time it had got my father down again. His throat was so torn that they all knew he was going to die.

"They carried him back to the castle. That evening my uncle, who'd not been with the hawking party, went to see my father in his room. The moment he came in Hero attacked him. I think he must have scented the wolf on my uncle's clothes. Anyway my uncle pulled out his dirk and killed him.

"My father . . . Hero was the dog he used to change with, you see. I don't know that for certain, but he must have been. He could hardly talk because of his throat, but there was a deadly quarrel, and I think my uncle must have said something which made my father guess what the wolf had been. I don't think till that moment he'd understood how jealous my uncle was, how he longed to be chieftain himself. To be chief of your clan, that's the finest thing in the world among us. There's been many and many a murder for it, and many more there'll be. But my uncle went raging out of the castle and nobody's seen him since.

89

"Next morning my father sent for me. My mother died when I was born, and he'd so grieved that he could not look at me. I had lived wild as a fox, almost, and I scarce remember him before that morning, lying under his window with the loch outside and the moors beyond, his face pale as linen and his brave beard hacked short for the bandages. He stared into my eyes a long while—I know now what he was looking for. He sent everyone from the room and made signs for me to fetch him a small oak chest. I hauled it across the floor to his bedside. He gave me a key and when I'd unlocked the chest he fumbled around and found a small packet, tight-sewn into cloth, which he gave me. He could not speak, but he made me understand with signs that I must keep it safe and secret and not open it till my wedding-day. Then he made me kiss him and sent me away.

"He died that night. I have not told you that all the business of the clan was in the hands of my father's steward, Michael. Next day Michael called the whole clan to a gathering. It took them three days to muster. There's a great stone by the loch, and it's there the clan gathers. Michael took me and stood me on the rock and told them that it was my father's command on his death-bed that I was to be chieftain, and they must swear their loyalty to me. They did not like it—they wanted a man like my father, who could lead them in war—but Michael told them that when I was old enough I would choose myself a husband from among them for that. Then the important men thought perhaps I would choose one of their sons, and he'd be the true chieftain, so they agreed. So the clan swore the old oaths they had sworn all my fathers, and I was chieftain.

"But the very next day Michael sent me away with six of our best men to guard me on the journey. He said it was my father's order that I must go to an abbey beyond the borders to get myself schooling and fit myself to be chieftain, but I think too he wanted to send me safe from the wolf.

"I was happy with the nuns. The abbess was my aunt, my mother's sister. She was a learned woman who could speak Latin and French, and Southron too, but she would speak with a child in our own good broad tongue, and sing songs with me in the language of our crofter-folk which is not the English at all. And I had my own dogs and pony, but I was never let ride far from the abbey without a guard.

"Michael came to visit me twice a year and tell me what was happening at home. It was all the wolf's doings. As soon as I was gone the whole clan had vowed to revenge my father's death and had tried to hunt the wolf, but it had been too clever for them. From the first it set out to kill the dogs which might track it. It took care to let everyone know what it was doing. It would come to a croft by night and take their dog and lay its body on the hearthstone, and if the crofter bought himself another dog it would kill that too, and by way of punishment it would take a bairn and kill it, or

90

murder all the man's cattle. Michael brought in hunting-dogs, but it trapped and killed them one by one. There was no end to the insolence of it. My father kept an old bear and dogs to bait it with. They kennelled outside the castle walls, and one winter night the wolf crept down and killed all five and dragged their bodies to the castle gate. Now there are no dogs in all my lands."

"It is afraid of dogs, then," said Hugh.

"Aye. That is my thought too."

"What about these two? Why has it not slain them."

"Boy has never set foot across the border. Lady only once. Let me gang on. When it had settled with the dogs the wolf began raiding. Raiding like any Highland thief. When my father was made chieftain there had been raiders all around our lands, but he had gone against them and destroyed them, tracking them into their lairs. I ken weel now how he did it, but others did not. It was for that the clan held him in respect, and now the raiding had begun again they started to say it was time to have a man for a chieftain, to go against the wolf and destroy it as my father would have done.

"That was my uncle's plan, I think. When the complaints were loud enough he would return. Perhaps he would kill the wolf, to prove his right . . . but if he reckoned so he did not understand what he was meddling with. I know this because when I change with Lady . . . och, Hugh, I canna tell you with words! You canna ken unless you do it your own self! It is the brawest feeling in all the world! Many and many a time I have been sore tempted to stay . . . only that I am chieftain of my folk, and I have my father's death I maun take vengeance for!"

Her voice rang and her hair flashed in the firelight as she tossed it back from where it had been hanging, veiling her bowed head as she told her story. She stared at the embers and went on more quietly.

"Only think," she said. "Suppose yourself to be my uncle. You have killed your own brother. Killed him for nothing. His child is chieftain. How can you live your life as a man after that? But there is another life. You can live as a wolf . . . do you understand, Hugh? My thought is that my uncle has almost forgotten why he goes raiding. He does it because he's a wolf. But he still has the wits of a man . . .

"Now, when I was twelve my aunt died and a new abbess was chosen who was determined to make me a nun. It was not for the sake of my own soul, mind you—it was so that the abbey would own my lands. First she had to break my will. She took away my dogs and would not let me ride out. She made me talk Southron and had me whipped for a word of our good broad tongue. She made me fast for my wickedness, days on end. Worst of all she would not let Michael see me. When he rode south she would tell him I was being punished—it was likely true, she would punish me for anything.

"They sometimes shut me up in a wee cell and left me for days, pushing in scant food to keep me from starving. All I had for comfort was my father's gift. I'd hide myself into a corner and take it out and prod and feel it, hours on end, until the stitching started to run, and I looked at it and told myself I could not keep my promise and wait for my wedding-day for either I would be made a nun and so never marry or else I would die. So I pulled it loose and saw what it was."

"The collar Lady wears?"

"Aye, with a paper explaining the secret. It was not for me, you ken? It was so that I could pass the secret on to my son when he was born, and a man would own it again. But I understood why he had gazed in my eyes so long before he made me bring him the chest—he was looking if he could see that I had the gift. You can sometimes tell, but it is not easy to be sure, looking with human eyes.

"Well, after that I thought long and long. First I unravelled how it maun be my uncle was the wolf. Then I knew it was only I could take vengeance. And then I began to think how I could escape from the abbey. I went to the abbess and told her that I had changed my mind and would be a nun, but not till I was sixteen, and I begged for my father's sake that I could have a wee greyhound to keep. She would not let me at first, but I was very obedient and careful and proper and in the end she let me choose myself a bitch, if I would write a letter to Michael saying I was to be a nun and he was not to come and see me more. Och, she didna ken our ways! Michael knew I would never write such a letter of my own will. His first thought was to raise the clan and make a great raid on the abbey to free me, but he couldna persuade the men to follow him so far. He was still arguing it when I got loose.

"Lady slept on the floor of my cell. In the wee hours I'd change with her and run about the abbey, prying and seeking. I made friends with the night porter by fawning on him, as though I was his own pet, and following on his rounds. One night when I saw he was well drunk I nipped the keys from his table and ran back to my cell and changed into my own body. I let myself out of the little wicket by the stables and took a horse and rode it away in the dark. I had no saddle, but I'd ridden bareback since I was a bairn. I'd neither food nor money so I hid in the woods all day and changed with Lady and hunted. That was when I first knew the pleasure of it. So I rode north six nights by the moon till I came to my own lands, where I stopped at the first croft and sent a message to Michael. I durst go no further for fear of the wolf.

"Michael rode out alone. His thought was that I maun go back with him to the castle and find myself a husband to be chieftain, but that was not my thought. First, I would be no nearer killing the wolf. Second, it is *I* am chieftain. It is *I* stood on the gathering rock and took the oaths. I ken weel how to hunt the wolf. I ken weel I maun have a man to do it for me. But I wilna give him my hand as the prize, and bear his babes and call him master. I maun needs do that if it is a man of my own folk kills the wolf. So I maun find me a champion from some other folk. In the abbey the nuns were aye gabbing of the noble knights in the court of the southron king, so I thought I would journey there."

"What did Michael say?"

"He didna like it at all. Whiles I thought he would carry me to the castle by force, but I told him that the wolf maun be my uncle, and that none of our folk could fight a warlock, but there were knights in the southron court who could do it. He didna believe me at first, but I told him about my father and Hero, and then he saw that it must be so. He still didna like it, but he saw I was willed to it, so he gave me money and let me go."

"So you came south to the King's court to choose a knight. Why did you do it the fashion you did? You could have come to the King in your own shape . . . and why did you choose me?"

She looked at him half-sideways, nerving herself for a crisis. She reached out and pulled one of her saddle-bags towards her.

"I told you the gift of changing runs in our kin," she said. "It was my thought that ours canna be the only kin. There maun be others, who dinna ken the secret. I thought too that I would see it better through Lady's eyes, and that was so. I kenned the moment I saw you, you were the one."

She pulled her hand out of the saddle-bag. She was holding a large black collar, twice the size of Lady's. She passed it across to Hugh. In the red fireglow he could not read the letters but his fingertips felt the line of indentations running along the inside of the leather from the buckle to the tail. They tingled under his touch. He shivered.

"I had it fashioned to fit Boy," she whispered.

They stared at each other over the embers. His heart was hammering again. He looked down to where his hands were turning the collar over and over. Slowly he started to undo the buckle. She reached across the fire and stopped him.

"To-morrow morn," she said. "First you maun put it round Boy's neck and let him wear it all one night. And there's another thing—you maunna ever let the collar slip from your human neck before you are safe changed back."

"What would happen?"

"I dinna ken."

"Very well, then. To-morrow morning."

Aaaah, the dew-smells and the stream-smells, the rich dark smell of wood-floor threaded with faint thrilling whiffs of the creatures that lived their secret lives among the trees, Lady's pleasant hairy scent, and the sourish reek of Hugh's own body where it crouched growling in front of him with the black collar round its neck. He shuddered his pelt, letting the hackles rise and lie flat, then trotted across the clearing and sniffed at the tussock the dogs had used the night before. The scents were sharp as names—Lady, Boy. As he lifted his leg and pissed on the tussock, renewing the message, he looked around. The wood seemed full of mist, its colours dim; horse and bush were almost the same shade of yellowish grey, hard to tell apart until the horse switched its tail. The movement made its shape suddenly clear, but as soon as it was still again it blurred into the bushes. Cynella had warned him that dogs see strangely, though she knew that only through Lady's eyes and greyhounds were bred to hunt by sight. Boy had been bred to trail by scent, and then to tackle a big wild animal face to face.

His hackles bristled along his spine at the thought and a snarl rumbled into his gullet. To release the tension he tried his new body, racing off into the wood, jinking among the trees. Birdsong twittered above him, a thrush on its branch singing the sun up. In sheer fun he leaped and snapped his jaws just below its perch, sending it darting away.

Lady came prancing up and challenged him to a tussle. They skittered among old leaf-drifts, whipping round tree-trunks. She snarled and nipped at his flanks. He caught her by the shoulder and rolled her clean over, growling deep in his throat. She curled her tail under her stomach in submission and he felt his own tail waving cheerfully behind him as he let her up. They raced back to the camp. He had been as quick as she was in the close twists of the scuffle but she was faster in straight flight. By the time he reached his human body Cynella was sitting up and taking Lady's collar from her neck.

Hugh bent his muzzle to his human face, licked and felt the shudder of change, like starting from a dream. He stood up, undid the collar and fastened it round Boy's neck. When he looked around he was shocked by the brightness, the sharp edges of the leaves, the glitter of dew, the clear colours. Deliberately he drew a long, enquiring breath. There were meanings there, he now knew, but too faint to read, savourless odours only.

Cynella stretched and laughed. There was a new feeling between them, a shared delight, secret to themselves.

"I havena played that fashion before," she said. "But it's braw, Hugh. Dinna you think so? Even alone it's the brawest thing in the world."

"Marvellous."

"We maun be canny, Hugh. Our bodies wilna guard themselves. The dogs dinna ken how to make them act, only dog-fashion. Och, look at poor Boy!"

Boy seemed dazed. He was snuffling at his fur and twisting his body about as though he thought some enemy had sneaked up behind him. Lady trotted over and licked his ears. He sniffed her but still looked puzzled until Hugh bent to scratch the back of the dark-furred skull. Boy sniffed carefully at Hugh's hands and legs, then shook the collar into place and seemed to forget that anything puzzling had happened.

And later that morning, as they were riding along the track Cynella said, "Look, Boy has changed masters."

Hugh glanced down. So far on the journey Boy had at best tolerated his company, and had tended to choose the further side of the path, with Cynella and her pony between him and Hugh. Now, though, he was trotting along in the shadow of Hugh's horse. What is more he immediately raised his head to meet Hugh's glance. Their eyes locked, and Hugh was aware of a strange bond that had not been there before. Boy was now part of him, and he of Boy. Their lives were joined.

Two evenings later they had a lesson in the very risk Cynella had talked of. They had camped in a lonely-seeming place. Hugh had gone hunting in Boy's body and had had the luck to find and pull down a yearling fawn only a few hundred yards from the camp. It was too far for a dog to drag, so he was trotting back with his mouth full of the satisfying warm richness of fresh blood when he heard a shout, more than one voice, and Lady's furious yelping. He broke into a gallop, reached the edge of the glade they had found, and paused. Straight across the clearing a man had Cynella gripped with her arm twisted up behind her back. Lady was darting at him, snarling and yelping, while he lashed at her with a club. Further along another man was wrestling with Hugh's body on the ground. Hugh leaped into the open and streaked across the grass. The man who held Cynella didn't see him coming, and was bowled clean over by the charge. He bellowed with pain as the wrist of the hand that held the club scrunched in Hugh's jaws, and then Hugh was on his chest with his muzzle at the man's throat.

"I have his club," called Cynella's voice. "Get the other fellow."

Hugh left the man lying and whipped away. He found his body trying to fight the other outlaw dog-fashion, pinning him down and nuzzling into his beard to get at his throat with his teeth. It would not have lasted. Just as Hugh came up the outlaw had managed to pull Hugh's own dagger from his belt and was working his arm into a position from which he could strike a death-blow. Hugh seized the fingers in his teeth and bit. The dagger dropped. He darted in and licked his own face.

The shudder of change. He was lying on the outlaw's body with his mouth full of reeking beard. Quickly he wrenched himself away and drew his sword. A look showed him Cynella standing over the other outlaw with the club poised ready and Lady snarling close by. He told his outlaw to roll over and lie flat on his face with his arms spread while he changed the collar to Boy's neck. Leaving Boy to guard the man he went over to Cynella, panting and shaking his head at his stupidity in ever having let this happen.

That night Hugh and Cynella stood guard, turn and turn about in the dogs' bodies. The outlaws lay lashed back to back and gave no trouble. They were in deadly fear of Boy. By the knightly code Hugh should have killed them, but he did not want that to be the first blood on his sword.

From then on they set up a routine. Each day's journey was limited by the need of the horses to graze, and also by the dogs' endurance; twenty miles was enough for Lady. So some time in the afternoon they would find a camp-site and let the dogs rest while they made it comfortable. Then Cynella would change with Lady and scout all around for dangers, hunting for supper at the same time, while Hugh rested. Then they would cook and eat and talk for a while, and as the fire died down Hugh would call Boy to him and change.

He stayed as Boy all night, mostly in a light watchful doze, but waking every couple of hours and roaming close to the camp under the trees, learning how to map the world of dark by sound and smell. There was more life in that dark then he would ever have guessed, owl-life and fox-life and the quick little lives of creatures that hide by day. If Boy's body was hungry and he chanced on one of these he would pounce and eat it, three quick crunches and a gulp, that being Boy's nature. One night he came face to face with a big dog-fox and instantly sprang to the attack, that again being Boy's nature, but when the fox turned and fled he did not chase it down, as Boy might have done, for fear of getting too far from the camp.

Well before sunrise he would wake Cynella with his muzzle and she would sit up and scratch behind his ears and then change with Lady, and in the bodies of their dogs they would play together. This was highly enjoyable, the finest sport Hugh had ever known. It was also important because it was practice, allowing him to learn all the powers of a big fighting dog, not only the strength and swiftness of Boy's marvellous body, but the instincts quicker than thought with which he was able to use it. Once in a real fight Hugh would need to let that side of his double nature take command; meanwhile he must find out with Cynella's help what was possible.

But he discovered as the days went by that this hour together, as the grey light turned silver and the silver gold until the sunrise glittered from every dewdrop, meant more to him than the joy of sport and the fascination of learning. It was something which without knowing he truly needed, a time of release from all the doubts and duties of knighthood, from the fret of to-morrow and the pang of yesterday, honour and shame, regret and hope, and all the burdens of thought, a holiday from being human.

Cynella, he knew, felt the same. They did not talk about it, but when they had changed back they would laugh together and she would toss her hair into place and stretch with remembered exhilaration before setting about the tasks of restarting the journey.

One morning, after more than a week of travel, they rode down into a handsome valley with a river running through meadows. There was no bridge but a ford, and close beside it a large yellow pavilion in front of which stood a table spread with food and wine. Half a dozen young men and women dressed in brilliant fanciful clothes strolled along the river bank. Three chargers were tethered by the pavilion. Three shields hung on poles close to the track. Hugh and Cynella reined up as they came out from the trees and studied the pretty scene.

It was something Hugh understood well. He was supposed to ride up to the shields and touch one with his lance, and then whichever of the men that shield belonged to would arm himself and joust with Hugh for the honour of his lady. When one was unhorsed the other would dismount and they would fight with swords until one confessed himself beaten. With the knights and ladies watching they would have to fight hard, and both would probably be well-wounded before one of them could honourably give in.

"You wilna fight?" whispered Cynella.

Hugh did not hesitate, though ten days before he would have been as eager as any of the men by the river to break lances and swap sword-thrusts. This was what his father had trained him for, his first real chance to earn himself knightly glory. He held out his mailed right fist and Cynella folded her hands round it.

"Madam," he said, "I give you my vow and oath that I will not for no cause of my own will and choice have ado with any knight in contest of arms nor partake of no other adventure whatsoever until that I have with God's help slain your enemy, your uncle."

"Thank you," she said. "I ken weel the cost, Hugh."

They rode down to the ford. Hugh dismounted and walked over to the table. The knights and their ladies came smiling to meet him. He explained his oath. The men were furious but managed to stay polite. The ladies were just as angry—what, this perfect day, the smooth turf, the feast, the pavilion, the shields and chargers ready, and to crown it all a knight coming by with his own lady with him. Everything just as it should be, and then the man won't fight!

"If so be that I return," said Hugh, "I will gladly have ado with each and all of you for my lady's sake."

The knights nodded and turned away.

"It will probably be raining," said one of the ladies.

"Or there'll be some other excuse," said another.

Hugh bowed to them and went back to Cynella.

"I'm sorry," she said as they spattered through the ford. "I ken weel the cost to your honour."

"My honour lies in finding and fighting your uncle," said Hugh.

It was true. Ten days ago the world of adventure had lain all round him, glittering with perils and marvels. Now it had narrowed to this single track, the road north, and at the end of it one dark foe. He heard a low growl and looked down to where Boy was padding in the shadow of his charger, hackles raised, head low, ears flat. Somehow he had felt Hugh's thought. He knew too.

The country became wilder, the villages further apart and ringed with wooden palisades. The few poor castles stood not among rich fields, but frowned from craggy ridges. Five nights after he had refused the fight at the ford Hugh in Boy's body was prowling the thickets above their camp when he crossed a new kind of scent-trail, sweet and greasy. He tracked it till he came to a pile of droppings which he recognised with his human mind from a description in a venery lesson. Bear.

And next day as they rode through pinewood Boy's low growl rumbled in the silence. All the dog's hackles stood straight, making a dark ridge. The ears were cocked, the head turned to peer into the pine-shadows. Hugh reined and sniffed the wind. Nothing. He slipped to the ground, put the collar round his own neck, changed . . .

Like a trumpet-note, an alarm from a tower, the message clanged through his mind. Wolf! He snuffled along the path and off into the wood, unriddling the criss-cross trails. Four grown wolves and two cubs, gone by in the dew-hour. He needed no remembered lessons this time—Boy's own instincts knew the enemy. Indeed the trail was like a call, a cry of love, telling him to follow, follow . . . Hugh had to will himself back to the others, to change and continue their journey.

Day followed day of dreary and difficult travel. True mountains began to rim the horizon. The farms were meagre huts, whose owners wore only lengths of rough cloth wrapped over one shoulder and gathered round the waist into a kilt. They used a language Hugh had never heard, though Cynella spoke it as her own. At last the path wound up a long hillside to the saddle of a pass. Here a small cairn had been piled by the roadside. Cynella reined her pony in and stood in her stirrups gazing north. She was flushed. Her green eyes shone. The chill north wind streamed in her hair.

"Look weel, Hugh!" she cried. "These are my own lands! Far as you can spy, and beyond!"

Hugh looked and his heart sank. Though he had not really supposed that Cynella's lands would be much like his father's few thousand acres—she had told him it took three days for the clan to gather—he had not in his heart understood the task, nor why the men of the clan, many of them skilled hunters, had found it impossible to band together and track down one wild animal. Now he saw. The area was not merely immense, folding away ridge after blue ridge to mountain peaks perhaps sixty miles off—and Cynella had said more lay beyond—it was also far, far wilder than any they had come through. They were looking north-west down a long vista between two chains of mountains, the one on the right curving away, its peaks and ridges marking the rough boundaries of Cynella's lands, but the one on the left being only, she said, the spine of those lands, beyond which the ground sloped away through country just as wild to a rocky coastline. The sea reached into the land through narrow forty-mile firths, breaking it up still further, and though in the distance the flanks of the mountains seemed to fall in smooth orderly sweeps, Hugh could see that this was an illusion. The slopes on either side of the pass were a jumble of gulleys and outcrops, boggy hollows, screes of immense boulders, and thickly wooded ravines. It would take a hundred men a year to search one mountain, and even then they would not be sure that they had probed every nook.

A mile down the pass stood a hovel. A woman came to the door and cried out. Two men came running round from the back of the hut as another woman and five small children rushed out. All of them gathered round Cynella's pony, babbling and seizing her stirrup to kiss her foot. She laughed and spoke to them. They turned and stared at Hugh in his suit of steel on his tall horse, as though he had been a monster brought by some travelling mountebank. They frowned at the dogs and spoke urgently to Cynella.

"They say we maunna let them out of our sight," she explained, "or the wolf will have them."

"How did they know who you are?"

"This was where I stopped when I ran from the abbey. But they would have kenned me without that by the colour of my hair."

She had to dismount and be friendly for a while, so Hugh did the same. He ate a salty oatcake and drank a minute cup of a fiery brown liquor the crofters distilled, but their hosts were clearly uneasy at the presence of the dogs, and glad when they rode on. It was the same at the next croft and the next—the passionate wild greeting of the chieftain, quickly replaced by fear and sullenness as the crofters began to sense that the wolf might punish them for letting a dog onto their lands. Without knowing the language Hugh sensed their fear.

So at the third croft Cynella asked and was told of a cave not far from the track a few miles on. Here they made camp, sleeping in the dogs' bodies at the cave mouth, turn by turn alert, with the horses tethered close and the human bodies resting safe within.

In the chilly northern dawn they played briefly round the cave mouth, breaking off every few seconds to raise their muzzles and sniff the wind and listen prick-eared. But freedom was gone. They both knew it and by common consent broke off their game, groomed each other's faces with their tongues and went and woke their human selves.

"We shalna do that for many and many a day," said Cynella as they stood at the cave mouth with the dogs nuzzling against their legs.

Hugh nodded. He felt too sad to speak.

As if to mark the change the crofter who had told them of the cave came marching up the hill to join them, carrying a long sword and a small round shield. All that day as they travelled they gathered retainers. At each hut a man would pull his weapons out from the rafters, pick up a bag of oatmeal and add himself to the escort. That night twelve of them held a rough feast out on the hillside. Two of the men had brought bagpipes on which they played sad music under the stars. It was pleasing to see the clansmen's pride at being with their chieftain, and their admiration that she should be content to sleep out in the heather wrapped in her blanket like a soldier.

Hugh lay awake a long while, brooding on the task ahead. Slowly he began to see that it was not so hopeless as he had feared. He was not going to have to hunt for a single wolf through this huge and difficult terrain. A lone wolf could roam vast tracts and lair where it willed, but this wolf was not like that. It had a human body to think of too. It had exactly the same problem Hugh and Cynella had had on their journey. Hugh remembered the fight with the outlaws, and how useless his own body had been with only Boy to guide it. So Cynella's uncle must have some way to keep his human body safe when he was out marauding as a wolf. A wild creature lived in that body then, so he would need to chain it up. In a cave, somewhere. There were probably many good caves among the mountains, but the magician could not use them all. To change lairs he would need to travel in his human body, with the wolf on a chain. He had lived years alone, so he would have goods to carry, surely. It would not be easy to change lairs. And more than that—a simple cave would not be enough. What if some other wild animal, or some man, chanced by when the wolf-body was away? No, he would need to be able to block the cave mouth, somehow open or close the place while he was in his wolf body . . .

And another thing—he could not leave his human body long. Two nights with a day between, perhaps. Yet he had spread terror through this whole huge tract. So his lair could not be on its fringes . . .

Then again, what did the human body eat? An endless diet of wild meat brought home by the wolf? After a while you would sicken on such food, surely . . .

And then there was the long, deliberate killing of dogs. Was that an aspect of the magician's madness, brought on perhaps by the murder of his brother and the death of gallant Hero? Or was it part of his plan of defences? Both, perhaps . . .

Well, at least there were things to be done, ways of beginning . . .

Next noon as they crossed a ridge their escort—twenty men now with a dozen wild urchins—broke into excited babble. Below them the hillside plunged to an iron-grey firth that twisted between the mountains towards the western sea. On a spit of rock rose a small grim castle, two towers of dark granite with a curtain wall running between them, a lower wall along the water's edge, roofs of purple slate, tiny glassless windows. Up the track from the castle a small procession was coming, five men on shaggy ponies, two pipers, a dozen men on foot carrying the same long swords and round shields as Cynella's escort. The riders wore only a slightly better version of the crofters' scant costume, with coarse linen shirts and blankets of finer weave pinned by a big silver brooch at the shoulder. They leaped down as the two processions met and ran to Cynella's side, where each in turn they seized her stirrup and kissed her foot. All their followers paid the same homage.

Hugh had dismounted and was standing aside, watching the ritual, when one of the riders strode up and stared him in the face, a short broad-shouldered man with wide-set green eyes, and with beard and hair that might once have been the same colour as Cynella's great mane but were now dulled with grey. Hugh held out his hand. The man hesitated, then gripped it hard, more to test its muscle than in greeting or friendship.

"I am Hugh de la Motte, Knight."

"I am Michael son of Michael son of Iain, Steward."

"You have been my lady's very good friend."

"*Your* lady's?"

"Only that I have promised to fight in her cause."

"You have come to hunt the wolf. Men as good as you have failed."

"Perhaps I will be fortunate."

"Fortune you will have need of."

The green eyes stared at Hugh. He did not need learning or knowledge of the world to read the signal—human instinct, as certain as Boy's recognition of the wolf-trail, knew the look of jealous fury. Well, it was natural, and perhaps it could be overcome.

There was a low rumble by Hugh's knee. Boy was unused to strangers.

Michael glanced down.

"Guard your hound well, sir," he said. "Dogs live no long life in these mountains."

"So I hear," said Hugh.

Hugh took the advice. While they were in the castle he fed Boy with his own hands, made him sleep on the floor of his bleak little room. When they rode out he kept him leashed at his side and Cynella did the same with Lady, but sometimes as they moved between the far-scattered crofts he changed with Boy and quartered the hillside, while his body, collared and leashed, strode steadily along by Cynella's pony. Only once or twice on these roamings, and then very faint and old, did he think he had caught any whiff of wolf-scent.

His plan of campaign was straightforward. He would work methodically down the main spine of mountains, visiting each croft and asking questions. He needed Cynella with him for this, as she spoke the crofter's language, and being their chieftain could command the truth from them. He could not take anyone else with him as that would prevent him from changing with Boy as he needed. The men in the castle, especially Michael, strongly resented their chieftain riding out with only this foreigner for escort, and there had been furious arguments. Cynella, head high, eyes blazing, had insisted on her own right to do as she wished, and had won. But at a cost. The men's pride was hurt, and more than their pride. They existed to be their chief's retainers. They had waited years for her return. Now she had come, and chose to ride round her lands without them, taking this insolent tall foreigner instead. Hugh found that he moved as warily among the narrow corridors and stairs of the castle as he did when he roamed as Boy along the hillsides.

Out among the crofts things were simpler, but still not easy. The people here were joyful to greet their chieftain, but terrified by the presence of the dogs, so usually Hugh waited with Lady and Boy out on the heathery slopes while Cynella rode into each croft alone. She came back to him with the same tales of horror and loss, flocks of sheep wantonly slaughtered, heifers pulled down in broad daylight, babies snatched from the box where they slept in the sun, and every dog killed. But for the last month, nothing. It seemed almost as though the wolf had known Hugh was coming, and was determined to leave no fresh trail.

Cynella also asked about caves in the crags above, and Hugh noted them down for Boy to explore later. No croft reported the loss of any human food.

For a week they worked along the slopes of Ben Affin, then moved south to Ben Moran. It was the same here at croft after croft until one afternoon they came to a bleak little holding high up a spur of the mountain, a place so isolated that the two brothers who farmed it and the wife they shared often saw no one but each other for weeks on end. So isolated that the wolf seemed to have left it alone. The brothers swore that they had not lost one lamb, except to foxes or eagles. Their children played about their door unwatched. But they kept no dog, and, Cynella said, they were afraid.

"It was strange," she said. "I do not think they were afraid of the wolf. They were afraid of me."

There are limits even to a large dog's strength, so next day they rested. Cynella told Michael that Hugh had a fever and would stay in his room. In the evening she took the dogs for a stroll along the lake shore, and came back with only Lady. She said Boy had run away. Michael said she would be lucky to see him again.

But next morning she went out with Lady and came back with Boy as well. On her way into the castle she met Michael feeding the old bear her father had kept for baiting. It was a mangy, sad old brute, whose chest-bones had been broken with hammers when it was a cub to weaken its deadly hug, but it was a matter of pride that the castle should have a bear at all.

"So he came back," said Michael.

"He must have spent the night hunting," said Cynella. "He's weary through."

"Fortunate he didna meet with the wolf."

"I think he would have given as much as he got."

"He has lost his collar."

"He wasna wearing one."

Michael turned from the bear-cage and stared at Boy, who met his gaze and then, far more friendly than usual, edged forward and sniffed at the hem of his kilt until Michael slapped him away with the back of his gauntlet. Boy did not snarl, but backed off and went obediently with Cynella into the castle and up the twisting dark stairway to Hugh's room.

"They leave a sack of oatcakes in the corner of a field," said Hugh. "It had been there about four days, from the smell. A man had come out several times to look at it. They have done this a long while—the path to the place was clear."

"But you didna smell the wolf?"

"I could not be certain. The field has a stone wall, and I thought I could smell a very faint old trail along the top of it, where a dog would not follow. The wall crosses a stream. He could jump down into that and go all the way up it to the peaks."

"Aye. My uncle might have come to them in man-shape and told them what they maun do, and what would befall them if they didna do it. But where has he gone, Hugh? Why has he made no raids?"

"I do not know. I think I must go back to Ben Moran. I may have to spend several days there. You can tell your folk my fever is no better."

"Aye. And if a body comes in to the room he will find you raving."

"Do not let anyone in, Cynella. There are men in this castle who would not be sorry to see me dead."

"They wouldna dare!"

"I think they would. You told me yourself there had been many a murder done for the chieftainship."

She stared at him.

"*You* would be chief?" she whispered.

He shook his head, smiling at her shock.

"That is why you came south for your champion, you told me," he said. "So that you would not have to pay him that price. But I do not think your men here understand."

"No more they do . . . I will guard you well, Hugh. Mind, I think from the way he spoke by the bear-cage Michael has guessed what Boy was doing so long away."

"So do I. Tell me, do you know what happened to Hero, your father's dog? Where was he buried?"

"In my father's own grave, and wearing . . . No, Hugh! They wouldna dare!"

"I think some of them would dare anything to be chieftain."

"It is Michael Steward you're thinking on. Michael!"

"You never told me that he was your kin."

"Own cousin to my cousins."

"You have never looked at him through Lady's eyes. He has the gift, Cynella."

"But you smelt naught on his kilt?"

"The bear-scent was too strong."

"No. It canna be true. He couldna make use of Hero's collar—there is no dog to change with in all these mountains, nor wolf forbye. My uncle killed them all."

"No doubt that is why he did it."

The rockfall reeked of death. It had taken Hugh three days to find the place, a low cliff at the side of a gulley far up Ben Moran. He nosed around the slopes. There were faint old man-smells here and there—a flat rock where fires had been lit, a smoothed place by the stream where someone might have knelt often to draw water, a cleft from which rose the smell of old cooked bones.

He padded back to the fallen rocks and with his dim-seeing eyes studied the cliff above them. No, there was nowhere up there that the rockfall could have slithered from, which meant that the boulders had never fallen. They had been carried and placed here to look like a rockfall. Man's work. No animal, however intelligent, could have done it. But an animal would need to be able to come and go, to open and close.

Nosing the heap where the reek was plainest Hugh found one large round boulder wedged in place by a smaller one. There were faint scrape-marks on the rock below, showing where the stones had been moved, many times. He hooked a paw round the smaller stone and pulled it clear. The big one was now balanced, and rolled easily aside when he nudged it. Behind lay a dark cavity which stank. Silence.

He backed off and peered all round. Through Boy's eyes all the slopes of the valley were mottled vague masses of yellowish greys and browns, but nothing there moved. The mild breeze carried no smell of dog or wolf or man. His pricked ears caught no signal. With hackles erect he nosed into the darkness.

Close inside the hole he found the source of the reek, the body of a large wolf. It had been dead about a month, savaged at the throat. It had been old before it died, with the muzzle round the yellow fangs almost silver. By the way it lay it seemed to have been stuffed into the cave through the hole, and the boulder then rolled shut behind it.

Hugh stepped across the body and paused. In the almost dark dog-sight saw clearer than man-sight could have done. Slowly he inched his way on. The dim light from the hole showed him a crude table and a three-legged stool. On the table were mouldy oatcakes. Piled against the wall by the table were weapons—long sword, round shield, hunting-spear. Then a lidless chest, with some blankets. Two cooking-pots and a water-jar. Last, right at the back of the cave, a bed of cut heather, and lying face down on it the body of a man. There was a collar round his neck. An iron chain led to a shackle in the wall.

It was too dark here even for dog-sight. Hugh had found the corpse by its smell, though it had not yet started to rot. The wolf had been dead about a fortnight longer. Gently he took the outflung fore-arm in his teeth. Between the stretched skin and the bone there was no flesh at all. The man had starved to death. Someone or something had killed the wolf outside the cave, had pushed the body back through the hole, and had then rolled the closing boulder back into place. Why had the killer not come in and killed the man? Because . . .

As Hugh's mind was groping towards the answer the silence was broken by a scrape and the clap of stone on stone. The light from the hole blanked out. A scrape, a rattle, a deep grunt which had nothing to do with rocks

or earth. By now he was at the entrance. Smell showed him the place. He put his muzzle beneath the balanced rock, hunched his hindquarters, heaved. Nothing. Not that way.

Another rattle and a chink vanished. Grunts and faint padding noises. The sound of another stone being trundled across to strengthen the barrier.

He stood an instant longer studying the problem, then darted back into the cave, picked up the stool in his teeth and laid it on its side about eighteen inches from the entrance-stone. He adjusted its position with his muzzle then went back and fetched the spear. It was about seven foot long with a stout shaft and a stubby point which he slid in below the balanced rock. Carefully he lifted the shaft and settled it in the angle of the stool where the upper leg joined the seat. Now he had a lever. He went back, crouched, eyeing the spear-butt, just visible by the light that came through chinks in the rock-barrier. He leaped once for practice, closing his jaws behind the butt.

Then he leaped in earnest, neck-muscles loose but all the rest of his body in tension to fling his weight up. His teeth clamped on the butt. He let his neck pivot with the movement of his body, then braced it as his weight came down. His hind legs were hunched in as though he had been jumping an obstacle, so that his weight would have room to fall.

The spear jarred in his jaws. Instinct had closed his eyes, but he forced them open and saw the rock jump. Light streamed through the widening gap, but then the spear-point began to slip and swing sideways. Hands might have held it steady but jaws were unable to control it. All he could do as the rock began to fall back was to wrench his neck sideways, thrusting the spear-point between it and its neighbour. It held, trapped between rock and rock. He took a fresh grip and flung his full weight back. As the rock rolled out and away, he sprang for the hole.

Something hard buffeted into his shoulder, twisting him sideways, but his momentum carried him through and he was free and bounding down the slope. Twenty yards clear he turned to face his enemy.

It was the castle bear.

The big beast came hurling at him down the slope, trying to finish him off before he had recovered his balance, but he was ready and sprang to one side, letting the rush of its charge carry it past and then whipping in to grip the thick neck from behind. The bear bellowed and lost its footing, tumbling head over heels towards the stream, and Hugh had to let go or be crushed.

In the middle of the shallow rushing water the bear rose on its hind legs to face his attack, and he paused. The creature was old, and crazed with its long cage-life. With its broken chest-bones its hug was little danger, but its claws were like iron and its snarling jaws savage still. Unless he let it trap him, pin him down and bite out his throat, it could do him little harm. No doubt that was how it had killed the wolf, catching it unawares as it came out of the cave. But it could not then get its bulk through the entrance to murder the man, so it had left him to starve.

But if Hugh was in no great danger from the bear, it also was safe enough from him. When he had bitten its neck his big incisors had barely pricked the thick bristly hide, and found a protective layer of fat beneath. It would take more than bites to finish off such an animal. He circled his enemy in silence, keeping the bear busy with darting rushes, letting the dog's lightning reactions control his movements while his man-mind thought the thing through.

Michael. It had to be Michael. Cynella had told him about the collars. He had dug at the grave and found Hero's. There were no dogs in the land, so he had tried with the bear and it had worked. Like Hugh, once he had known that the wolf had a human body to protect, he had been able to narrow the search. A bear's sense of smell would be at least as good as a dog's. He had found the cave, and killed the wolf.

Why had he not then gone back to the castle, to his human body and announced his triumph? His whole motive, Hugh was sure, was to marry Cynella and become chieftain. Even his wild scheme to raid the abbey and free her had had this as his aim. He had been dismayed when after her escape she had told him she was going south to find a champion. He had been furious with jealousy when she had returned with Hugh. Perhaps he had not wanted to claim her till she was alone in the castle, surrounded by men as loyal to him as to her. He had decided to wait for the champion to fail. And then at the bear-cage he had realised that Hugh, as Boy, might find the cave after all, so he had come himself also and lain in wait . . .

Had he come alone? Michael, like all who worked the magic with the collars, had one deadly weakness, the need to safeguard a human body. Had sullen, secretive Michael trusted some accomplice? No! The bear could not lie in wait at the cave alone—its eyes were too poor, and if it came close its scent would betray it . . . Somewhere then out on the hillside, down wind, not too far off . . .

Three times more Hugh circled, snarling and rushing, tensing as if to leap for the throat and then backing away again. Behind the bear's furious piggy little eyes he sensed now the human mind, reasoning the problem through as he had done, searching for escape from the stalemate.

Now he leaped in earnest, but not at the bear. Instead he sprang past it and raced on up the slope towards the cave. Muzzle to earth he zig-zagged. There! Plain as a path the greasy sweet bear-trail. He loped along it, slantwise up the hill.

The bear, taken by surprise only for an instant, was galloping up the stream, beginning to climb the hill. Hugh stretched his long legs to full running. Though he was far faster than the bear, he would still have a minute at most.

The body lay prone, growling, chained to a boulder in a fold of steep heather at the top of a scree. Hugh leaped and landed square on its shoulders. His teeth nipped the collar and he wrenched it round to find the buckle. The collar was made of coarse dark leather, far too large for any dog, but he could feel that there was a narrower ridge inside.

The body heaved beneath him. He hung on, flung his weight down, knocked the body flat, got his incisors under the leather and wrestled the tail of the collar through its loop. The body heaved again, flinging him clear. He sprang and caught it off balance as it started to rise, barging it flat on its back, and then pounced again.

This time the body made no attempt to throw him off. Instead the arms closed round his shoulders, hugging him closer as the mouth nuzzled for his neck. He let it do what it wished, craning round again for the buckle. Human teeth ground into a fold of skin and fur. He endured the pain, feeling with his tongue for the brass tang. There. He slid an incisor under the tang and hoicked it out of its hole, then took the whole buckle in his mouth. The body snarled beneath him, the arms hugged cracking close, the teeth explored for a vein. Slowly he inched the buckle clear of the tail.

The moment he felt it free he bucked with all his strength, wriggling himself down out of the hug. The teeth lost their grip and he was free. He pranced away up the hill with the collar dangling from his mouth. It tasted of earth and death—Hero's old collar, now sewn along the inside of the bear-collar, had lain years in the grave.

With an agonised wheezing the bear climbed the hill. Manbody rose to meet it. Bearbody rose too, teetering on stubby legs. Hugh's plan had been to take the collar as a hostage, as proof of what Michael had done, so that he could not return to the castle with some human lie on human lips to explain his absence. But now, as the two bodies rushed together, he remembered what Cynella had said when he had held his own black collar for the first time in his hand—he must not ever take it off his human neck until he was safe changed back with Boy. As the two bodies rushed together he sensed, through Boy's animal awareness and not his human mind, a new presence on the hillside, the soul of all wildness whirling loose. Mad.

Bear bellowed, man howled. The bodies met. They grappled, lost balance and locked in each other's grip went crashing down the scree.

Hugh found them thirty yards down, still clasped chest to chest. Neither moved. There was no sign of a wound. Perhaps Michael's head had been caught on a rock, but surely the bear's skull was too tough for that to harm it. Very cautiously he nosed in and sniffed at their faces. No breath stirred. He backed off and lay tense, watching, while the shadows moved among the rocks. After a full hour he decided they were indeed both dead.

In the room where her father had died, high up in the tower, Cynella stood at the small square window and looked out over the loch. All along the shore the clan was gathering, the last remote crofters coming in. Pipes wailed in the morning mist. Hugh watched over her shoulder. Behind them the dogs lay on the floor, Lady licking gently at Boy's torn neck. Boy did not seem puzzled by the wound. It was there, and he had no need to remember how he had got it.

"What shall I be telling them, Hugh?"

"Say that Michael found and killed the wolf. Say he used the bear to track it down. Tell them that the same enchantment that had allowed your uncle to change his shape somehow killed them too. All that is truth. I would bear witness. I was there."

"You will stand beside me on the rock?"

"They would not understand my speech."

"Yet you could stand beside me. You have the right."

"You are their chieftain and no one else."

She had not looked at him, but he had felt her tension, like that of a trapped wild creature. Now she turned, squared her shoulders and tossed her hair back to stare him in the face, just as she had the first time they had met.

"You have the right, Hugh."

"But you do not wish it with your heart, I think. Your honour tells you that you must make the offer."

"And you dinna want it?"

In spite of her relief, she was hurt too, and not only in her pride. Hugh, unlike her, had already thought all this through in his careful way, and knew what he felt.

"I do not wish to live here and be chief, or the chief's right hand. Your people would never understand or respect me, and they would despise you for choosing a foreigner. If you could come and live with me in my own lands, when I have won them with my sword . . ."

"I canna, Hugh. I maun bide here."

"But you do not want to either, I think."

"No . . . Och, Hugh, if only we could be Boy and Lady always!"

They laughed together and she went down the stair and out onto the shore to face her people.

Very early next morning, as the dark began to silver, they stole out with the dogs upon the hillside and changed bodies and played for the last time together and then came back before the castle woke. Later that day Hugh rode south with Boy loping beside him wearing a different collar. He had deliberately left the magical one behind. All that was over. He would not even, he thought, care to tell the court the tale of his adventures. They would find it amusing, no doubt, but what had he done that they would understand or think honourable? Lived for a while in the body of a dog and watched a bear and a traitor kill each other. Well, perhaps he would find some knightly glory on his journey south. He could start with those three fellows at the ford, if they were still there.

But, as one of their ladies had said, it would probably be raining.

Again he drifts up through the pool of oblivion, touches the surface, wakes. The pool vanishes. Beneath his naked shoulders he feels the naked earth. Earth is his last robe. Once he wore the pelt of a bear and laired in a hollow tree. Once he wore shreds of coarse sacking and strode the high ridges. Once he wore fine wool dyed seven colours, boots soft as the skin of a bride, gold three fingers thick around neck and elbows, beads of amber in his hair, and stood beside the High King.

Memory rebuilds the moment, the High King throned on the man-built hill, himself at the High King's elbow, below them the Nineteen Kings of the island, beyond those, spreading out across the plain, the tribes. All come to one man's summons.

Nineteen kings for the nineteen tribes. These were not the young Kings of the Year, chosen to rule from one great Rite to the next and then to die —these were kings who would rule as long as they could grip war-axe, some young, some scarred with time and battle, but man-slayers all, their smile wealth, their frown death. The King of the Otters ruled from Blacksands to Umba's River; eight thousand fighters gathered to his muster; for nine years he had knelt to no other king. The King of West Cats ruled one sparse valley and could call thirty-three men to his war-pole; for nine years he too had knelt to no other king. But now both knelt on the slope of the man-built hill while their tribes watched in silence.

For nine years no High King had ruled. No one had sat on the Stone Chair. Like baiting dogs the tribes had warred mindless. Sometimes one king had decided he had gained mastery enough and had issued the summons and travelled with henchmen and allies to the man-built hill, but before they had reached it they had lost their way among the marshes. There were mists, there were fevers. Guides who had been there before forgot the route. Paths circled back on themselves. So the kings had returned to their holds and allowed themselves to be persuaded that the time had not been ready. What use to find the hill and to sit on the Stone Chair unless they could hold in their right hand the axe Iscal, and that was lost in the Bog of Beara? The last High King was dead, his line all slaughtered, and Iscal lay deep in black ooze. There would never again be a High King, only endless warfare.

Then, on the self-same day, in nineteen holds many days' journey apart, a man had stood suddenly in each king's hall where he feasted with his fighters. The man's robe was of fine wool dyed seven colours, there was gold three fingers thick around neck and elbows, beads of amber in the wild hair. In a masterful voice, using each king's secret name, he had cried to that king to come at the next full moon to the man-built hill, and then he had vanished.

So the kings had come, bringing fighters and elders. They had found no mist and no fevers. They knew the way without guides. Along straight paths they travelled to the man-built hill and found, sitting on the Stone Chair, a boy. In his right hand he held a war-axe. Its haft was twisted yellow sea-ivory, its double-bladed head was black obsidian polished smooth. There was no weapon like it in all the island. They knew its name without asking.

Though they did not yet know his name, they knew the boy also. Too young for a fighter but recognisably a child of the true line, somehow saved from the slaughter, somehow rescued and nurtured by the man with amber in his hair who now stood by his side, the man who had caused the axe Iscal to float up through the ooze, who had twisted the paths about the man-built hill, who had waited and watched until the boy was ready, and then had cried in their holds and brought them here.

So they had come, and seen, and known what they saw, and had knelt unbidden before the Stone Chair . . .

He remembers the silence, the wonder, the sunlight. He remembers the softness of wool across his shoulder-blades. He wears an even richer robe now, a cloth that all people earn in the end. He wears the turning world.

The pool of oblivion wells up round him. He lets himself drift down. On the under-surface the image of his memory, the image of the High King, ripples, changes, becomes his dream . . .

HEN Lord Alfin's soldiers came Ceri was deep inside the holly-tree, looking for the egg the yellow hen used to hide there. She heard Bran's wild barking cut suddenly short, a scream from her mother, a shout from her father, fear and outrage in all three voices. She climbed the first few branches of the holly to a place where she could see out through a slot of leaves. Four soldiers in pointed helmets held her parents pinioned. Her two small brothers watched white-faced and wide-eyed. Bran's body lay stretched on the ground.

Ceri's father was struggling and shouting. She could hear his words.

"You cannot do it! We hold from the King!"

She had heard him say the same words so often as he pushed back his chair after breakfast—"Well, my darlings, we hold our land by ancient right direct from the King, and Lord Alfin cannot take that from us however much he wants to close the forest for his hunting. But rights are not riches and we must work for our living."

Then they would go out and work all day on the farm, feeling safe in their rights. But now when Ceri's father bellowed the words as though they were some magical charm to drive the soldiers away, the chief soldier only laughed, and turned and gave orders. Then other soldiers lit twists of straw and started to set fire to the farm.

When they had gone, driving her family ahead along with the pigs and the cows as though they were all animals like each other, Ceri crept out of the holly tree and looked for food. She found some young carrots in the vegetable patch and a stale loaf which had been put out to feed to the hens. There were five eggs in her basket. She knew the place where her father kept what he called his hoard for desperate days, so she waited till dusk in case anyone was watching and then dug at the back of the pear-tree and found the jar. She took out three silver pennies and buried the jar again and smoothed the place carefully over.

Next morning Ceri set out to look for the King.

It was a long and frightening journey through a ruined land. There were bands of soldiers on the roads, wild as wolves, looting and burning. There were deserted villages and towns with half the houses roofless. And there were grim castles, small and large, where the local war-lords tried to hold their own lands fast and wrest their neighbours' from them. When Ceri asked where to find the King, people laughed at her, or sighed, for her and for themselves.

At last, with no food left and only one silver penny still hidden in the hem of her skirt, she trudged up a grassy path that wound between steep hills. The path levelled and started to fall. She came out into the open and saw the end of her journey.

It was dusk, with a big moon rising. In another night it would be full. Below her lay the sea, stretching from the darkening east to the still burning west. The land ended in cliffs. The path wound down to a promontory on which stood an enormous castle, large as a town. Even in the gathering dark and at this distance Ceri could see that it was a ruin. She sat down by the road and for the first time in all her journey wept.

"What is the matter?" said a voice.

Ceri looked up and saw a man standing in the middle of the path. As far as she knew there had been no one following behind her and she had seen no one coming up the path ahead, so it seemed that he must have come out of the bare hill. He was small and pale, but with dark eyes, and dressed in a long green cloak trimmed with gold. Somehow he seemed not quite to be standing on the ground. Sadly Ceri told him her story.

"I don't know what to do," she said.

"You want my help? If you do, you must pay me. I give nothing for nothing."

Ceri fumbled in the hem of her skirt and took out her last silver penny. She had no use for it now. She didn't mind whether she lived or died. The man took the coin, balanced it on his thumbnail and flipped it in the air. At the top of its spinning arc it vanished.

"Look," said the man, and pointed towards the castle.

It had changed. Lights glowed in the windows. Sentries paced the battlements, calling their watch-cries under the rising moon. A hunting party rode in over the drawbridge and was welcomed by trumpets at the gate. A ship with one great striped sail slid over the still sea towards the harbour.

Ceri stared and stared. When she turned to thank the man in the green robe he was gone.

She ran down the path. There was mist below her, spreading along the shore-line. When she reached it it seemed almost as solid as a wall, but she groped her way through and came out into clear air. The castle was still there, alive, with its sentries pacing and calling. She expected to be stopped at the gate and asked her business but the guards did not seem to notice her, and when she went inside and asked the passers-by to tell her how to find the King they paid no attention. At first she thought this was because they were all too busy, but soon she found that they really could not see her or hear her, and when she held her hands up in front of her eyes, though she could see them she could see through them too.

Frightened now she wandered from courtyard to courtyard. Marvellous plants grew on the walls, filling the air with the scent of their flowers. Strange foreign trees rose among the buildings. Fountains gushed into stone pools. There were statues and monuments. The open spaces were lit by bright lanterns under which revellers went to and fro. Lovers sang beneath open windows. Everyone seemed rich and carefree.

At last, near the middle of the castle, Ceri came to a single great building with tall pointed windows which glittered in the moon and shone with bright colours from the lights within. She went inside and found an enormous hall, crowded with people in brilliant robes and jewels. Minstrels played from a gallery. Servants went to and fro with golden goblets. Ceri crept among the people, ashamed of her ragged clothes, but still they did not seem able to see her.

In the middle of the hall she found a clear space, roped off, in which a man sat on a gold chair. He wore a circlet of gold with three pale blue stones at the front. He looked young and strong. His eyes were the same colour as the stones in his crown. He was the King.

Two men stood in the cleared space in front of him. To judge by their clothes one seemed to be a great noble and the other a poor farmer, like Ceri's own father. There had been some kind of dispute between them which the King was being asked to settle. He listened to what they said and gave judgment. The farmer seemed pleased and the noble disappointed, but all who stood around listening nodded and smiled.

Then a herald cried aloud that the King's justice-giving was ended for the day, and he would now watch any who came to entertain him. There were jugglers, weird beasts, tumblers, dancers, and lastly a small man in a long green cloak trimmed with gold who showed the King a marvellous toy, a golden bird with rubies for eyes which stood on a crystal branch and flapped its wings and sang. The King was very pleased and signalled to one of his officials to give the man a bag of gold for his toy, but the man said it was not for sale.

At that the King grew angry and signalled again, and soldiers came and took the man away, but the King kept the golden bird and played with it. Ceri noticed the noble who had lost the dispute with the farmer frowning as he watched, and muttering behind the back of his hand to his neighbour.

Suddenly there was a noise like a harp-string twanging and being tuned tighter and tighter while it vibrated, till it snapped. The hall seemed to fill with mist, and then Ceri was waking out on the hillside on a brilliant morning. Below her lay the ruined castle, dark and sad against the sparkling sea. She felt in the hem of her dress but the penny was not there.

Because there seemed nothing else to do she walked down the path towards the castle. There was no wall of mist and the ruin stayed a ruin. When she reached it she found the drawbridge down, its chains rusted, its planks too rotten to trust. She balanced her way across on one huge old beam to a little door that sagged open in the grim gate. There were no guards or sentries. Instead of a challenge she heard only the shrieking of gulls, nesting on every ledge and sill. Inside was desolation. The immense outer walls might stand for centuries, but they were a shell and the life inside was gone, its remains crumbling away. Roofs had fallen in, windows were gone, mortar had loosened its hold on stone so that walls had started to tumble. Courtyards were blocked with brambles, though a strange foreign tree might still soar above the tangle, or a spring still trickle from stone lips into a basin.

But in spite of the ruin Ceri recognised her way. It was the same castle she had visited the night before, but now when she held her hands in front of her eyes she could not see through them. Picking her way through brambles, climbing over piles of rubble, she made her way to the hall where she had seen the King give justice. That too was in ruins, its roof fallen in, its tall windows empty of glass, but in one corner of it she found something new, a crude thatched hut huddled against the old stone walls. A rusty spade leaned by the door-post.

Inside, the hut was almost dark, and stank. There was an iron pot hanging over a fire of rotted timber, a table with a mug on it, a stool, and a pile of filthy bedding. Ceri thought the hut was empty, but then something snorted like a feeding sow, the bedding heaved and a man rolled out onto the floor. He crawled across to the stool, pulled himself up onto it and sat there hunched and groaning. After a while he reached down behind the table and picked up a big jar, which with trembling hands he tilted over the mug. It must have been nearly empty because he had to hold it upside-down before anything came out—a dark, sweet-smelling liquid at which he gulped greedily. He shook his head, spat, snorted and raised his head. For the first time he saw Ceri. He stared at her with pale blue, bloodshot eyes.

"Whaddyawan?" he snarled.

"I am looking for the King."

"You've found him."

"You?"

The man took another gulp at the mug, then rose and stood swaying. His clothes were rags, held in place with criss-cross lashings and splodged with spilt food, but the torn cloth glinted with threads of gold, and the lashings had once been silken cords.

"Me. King," he said. "All this. Mine."

He waved a wild arm, lost balance and clutched at the table to stop himself falling. Ceri gazed at him, appalled.

"Don't believe me?" he mumbled. "Show you."

He lurched away towards his bed, where he rootled like a dog among the bedding till he found what he wanted and turned. In his hands he held a circlet of gold with three pale blue stones at the front. He crammed it, crooked, over his tangled locks. Ceri couldn't tell whether he was the same King she had seen giving judgment. He might have been, or he might have been his great-great-grandson.

"Crown," he said. "Now you've seen King in his crown. Take a good look. Last chance to see King in his crown. Last chance anyone see him."

He slumped on the stool and stared into the mug.

"When's full moon?" he said.

"To-night," said Ceri.

"Thought so. Man comes to-morrow. Bringing last jar of wine. Give him crown to pay for it. Kept crown till the end. Nothing else left in treasury. Can't buy any more wine. Life not worth living, so jump over cliff. Thought it all out. Ready to go. No more crown, no more King. Finish."

He took the circlet off his head and turned it this way and that, smiling like a child at the glinting stones. Suddenly he began to weep.

Ceri woke in the middle of the night. The hut seemed to be filled with bright mist, which cleared, and she saw that the hut was gone and the brightness was moonlight streaming down into her face through a tall window glazed in different colours. She looked up and could not see the sky, because the hall had its roof again, dim-hung with banners.

Something moved, and a man walked into the patch of moonlight. It was the King she had seen giving judgment, but now he was armed for battle. She followed him as he stole down the hall, in and out of the strips of brightness where the moon slanted through the tall windows. In the shadows at the edge of the seventh patch he stopped, but Ceri, standing behind him, could still see him black against the silver shaft. He took his sword and prised up a small flagstone, then knelt and gently settled something into the hollow beneath. He fitted the stone back into place and stole away.

Mist bleared the moonlight. The note of the harp-string whined up the scale and snapped short, and Ceri was standing in the roofless hall with moonlight streaming down through empty windows and the hut back in its place. She went and picked up the spade from beside the door and walked down the hall counting the patches of moonlight. At the edge of the seventh patch she found a place where four huge flagstones had been laid in a pattern that left space for one small stone between them. Slowly she teased the grass out of the cracks around it until she could work the corner of the spade down and lever the stone out.

Below was a dark hole, filled with softness and rot. Things of the dark which made their homes there wriggled at her touch. At last she felt a hardness. She grasped it and pulled it out, holding it into the moonlight to pick away the rotted scraps of the velvet and ebony casket in which it had lain. As she cleaned it, it began to glitter in the silver light, crystal, gold and rubies.

Ceri took the bird back to the hut and put it on the table next to the mug. She had no real plan. Her hope was that the King might use it to buy his wine instead of his crown, and that would give him another month, during which he must surely sometime come to his senses enough to tell her what to do about Lord Alfin taking away her parents' rights.

Next morning, well before sunrise, the King rose trembling and groaning, staggered to the table and tilted the last mug of wine out of the jar. He gulped it down, wiped his mouth and then noticed the golden bird. He stared at it, blinking. A sly look came into his pale eyes. He slunk back to his bed, took the crown out from under his pillow and hid it deep in the filthy tangle of his bedding.

They breakfasted off stale cold slop from the iron pot, and then went out with the King carrying the golden bird cupped between his hands. He didn't seem to notice Ceri. She followed him through the ruined buildings to a platform at the cliff's edge where an immense stone stairway zig-zagged down to a tiny harbour. In the pale dawn light a ship was sliding in to the quay, furling its great striped sail as it came. Three men landed, two of them sailors carrying a wine-jar slung on a pole. The third, who led the way, was a small man wearing a long green cloak trimmed with gold.

The King waited, trembling and licking his lips. When the strangers reached the top of the stairway he rushed at them, holding the gold bird out in front of him. The man in the green cloak took it and examined it carefully, turning it to and fro. With his fingertip he touched what must have been a hidden spring, for suddenly the bird rose tip-toe on its branch, and flapped its wings and sang. The King watched anxiously, as though he was afraid the bird might not be precious enough to pay for a whole wine-jar, but at last the man in the green cloak nodded, unsmiling. The sailors put the jar down.

Immediately the King knelt beside it, clasped it to his chest like a lover, rose to his feet and staggered away. It was a large jar, and full, but despite what the wine had done to him he was still a big strong man. The wine-merchant looked at Ceri with dark unfriendly eyes. She did not know whether he was the same man she had seen on the hillside—somehow she could not remember quite what that man had looked like—but though the soles of his boots touched the paving he had the same odd look of floating in a different kind of space. Without a word he turned and led the sailors down the stairway.

Ceri found the King wrestling with the stopper of the jar. It was well sealed with wire bindings and wax, but at last he wrenched it off and tilted the jar eagerly over his mug. As the first liquid came he started, almost dropping the jar, but he settled it onto its base and peered into the mug with bulging eyes. He sniffed, then sipped.

With a wild, appalling cry he lurched to his bed, rooting for the crown. As soon as he'd found it he rushed out of the hut and staggered away through the ruins to the top of the stairway with Ceri running behind. They halted, gasping. The sun was just up, and far below the ship was heading out over the glittering sea, its striped sail full of the dawn wind and the man in the green cloak standing at the helm.

The King bellowed. He pranced and screamed and waved the crown beseechingly. The helmsman did not look round.

"Thief! Cheat! Murderer!" yelled the King.

He swung his arm back to fling the crown after the boat, but Ceri caught it and clung, shouting "No! No! No!"

All at once the energy drained out of the King. He groaned, hunched his shoulders and shuffled away with the crown dangling unnoticed from his hand. Back in his hut he sat on his stool, moaning. Out of sheer habit he picked up his mug and gulped.

"Water," he whimpered. "Wine all gone. Kingdom gone. Finish."

"You've still got your crown," said Ceri.

He sighed and put the circlet on his head.

"Halloo!" cried a voice outside. "Anybody seen the King?"

Dazedly the King rose and went to the door of the hut. Ceri peered round behind him. The rising sun was shining straight through the huge broken window at the eastern end of the ruin, but against the glare she made out a large man a few paces off. He stood straddle-legged, a brutal black shape with a lance in his hand. The sun glittered off the outline of his helmet and the strips of steel on his shoulders. Further away were more men, some with pointed helmets and spears. Ceri shrank back.

"You the King, then?" said the man.

"Uh . . . Uh . . ."

"Right. I've brought a document for you to sign."

"Duh . . . ?"

The man laughed in the King's face.

"Death warrant," he said. "These three fools. You sign and we'll string them up."

"Wha . . . What have . . . ?"

"No business of yours, King. Your job from now on is to sign death warrants when I tell you, that's all. Right?"

The King shuddered. It was not like a shiver from within, but as though some force around him were starting to batter him to and fro. The fit died, and as it did so one of his wild shifts of mood swept over him. He snatched up the spade from beside the door and charged, swinging the rusty blade in a flailing arc. The man leaped back, but not quickly enough. The blade edge caught him at the knee-joint. He bellowed and went down.

The King charged on. Against the sun-glare Ceri could not make out what was happening, and it was all over in an instant, but in that instant she heard the King roar. He seemed to have grown a foot taller. The sun blazed round him, with the square blade of his weapon whirling black overhead. A man fell, his helmet rattling across the flagstones. Cries, and a crash, and another man falling. The man who had spoken to the King was on his knees now, crawling towards the fight with a long knife in his hand. Ceri snatched up the stool by its legs, rushed out of the hut and brought the stool down with all her strength on the back of the man's neck. He collapsed with a grunt and lay still. She backed away and saw that the fight was over.

The King was leaning on his spade, gasping and shaking his head. Two soldiers, as well as the man Ceri had hit, lay still on the ground. A fourth soldier was kneeling with his own spear held at his back by a man with a halter round his neck. Two other men, also with halters, were struggling to free themselves from the ropes which lashed their arms behind them. Ceri took the knife and cut them loose.

They held a sort of trial, with the King for judge, sitting on his stool in the centre of the ruined hall. The man Ceri had hit, it turned out, was the leader of a band of freebooting soldiers who had settled on a group of villages to pillage and murder. The men with the halters were three brothers who had tried to organise the villagers to resist, appealing to them in the King's name to fight for their rights. The appeals still had some faint force, and the brothers might have succeeded if the soldiers had not captured them, and then, to show everyone else how useless such appeals now were, had brought them here to get the King's own name on their death-warrants. One of the brothers had managed to loosen his bonds unnoticed, and had taken advantage of the King's attack to surprise his guard.

Ceri was not sure how much of the story the King understood. He sat nodding and mumbling on his chair, and when the brothers asked for his judgment he waved a vague hand towards the cliffs. Two of the soldiers were dead already. The brothers took the other two away and then came back for the bodies.

While they were gone Ceri felt thirsty so she went into the hut and filled the King's mug from the jar and drank. It was only water, but tingling fresh, as though it had been drawn from a spring that rose from deep inside the hills. She filled the mug again and took it out to the King.

Sitting on his stool he sipped, and as he did so he looked at Ceri, seeing her for the first time, it seemed. A faint light began to glow in the pale blank eyes, but he said nothing until the brothers came back.

They had swords at their belts and were wearing the soldiers' leather armour and helmets. They must have been talking among themselves, for they knelt in a row in front of the King and put their hands between his and asked him to come back with them to their villages and be King of those few acres. He nodded and held up a hand.

"I will come," he said. "Something else first. This child came before you. Why did you come to the King, child?"

Ceri told him, and she was sure this time he understood, but when she had finished he sighed and carefully counted the three armed men now standing before him.

"Small army," he said. "Take time."

It took seven years. Back home the brothers told what the King had done for them, so other villagers took heart and armed themselves, and then a petty local Lord grew suspicious and came marauding, but mismanaged his campaign and lost his castle and lands, and slowly, slowly, the King's power grew. There were hideous battles, meadows drenched with blood, towns left burning, farm after farm empty and dead. Often all seemed hopeless, worse than the worst of the old days, but then, sometimes by courage, sometimes by skill, but mostly by sheer luck, the balance would tilt back.

On a summer morning of the seventh year Ceri stood at the doorway of her parents' half-rebuilt farm. She was wearing her wedding-dress and her mother was sewing the last lucky stitches into the hem when a trumpet blew and the Clerk of the King's Rights rode up with his guards and servants, and work on the dress had to stop.

The Clerk was going round the kingdom, now that it was at peace, checking that all the ancient rights were held by their proper owners, wherever they could be found after the years of chaos. He was a proud and important man, more used to dealing with nobles and mayors of towns than with single poor farmers, but the rolls said that for some reason Ceri's parents held their farm direct from the King, so there were new deeds to be read and sealed. In the middle of the business the Clerk noticed Ceri in her wedding-dress, and asked and was told that she was to be married next day. He was not a generous man, but he knew the King took a particular interest in this small holding, so, hoping to please his master, he told one of his servants to give the girl a present.

Everyone else was busy with the documents, so only Ceri saw what happened. The servant came over, a little man wearing a long green cloak trimmed with gold. This time she was almost certain he was the man who had seemed to come out of the hills above the ruined castle seven years ago. He had exactly the same floating look, as though his world was not the same as our world, but somehow alongside it, invisible, but he did not smile and gave no sign that he recognised Ceri.

He held out his empty hand in front of her. In the air a coin appeared and dropped in a spinning arc into his palm. He gave it to her and turned away without a word.

It was a silver penny. Ceri kept it as long as she lived.

Dreams are their own masters. However large and strange the mind, however long and still the dark, still the dreams come and go, unwilled. They are like bards, wandering from feast to feast, coming out of the night into the long wooden hut where a chieftain rewarded his fighters with mead and roast meat to amuse the company with their stories.

There was a dream on his way to waking, filling the hall of his mind with its images, but now he does not remember the dream. Instead he lies in the silence, remembering bards.

The wonder-bringers, the knowers, the tellers of the marvellous acts of gods and the deaths of heroes, the praisers of men. Quick to sing the glories of the chief on whose stool they sat, admired for the extravagance of praise—a fighter must boast for himself, but a chief has others to do his boasting. Bards who in three words could make a fighter's name a by-word, for courage or for cowardice.

And bards of another kind, holy, with secret knowledge. Bards who would stand suddenly before a king and speak, without harp, without chanting, speak not of battles fought long ago, but battles yet to happen, or happening now, far off, under different skies, the vision flooding into the mind unwilled.

He had that knowledge and power too. He stood once in a chief's hut and saw in his vision the thatch blazing and the fighters slaughtered around the tables. He stood once by a queen's well and saw the ship that at that very moment was grinding into the shingle of a distant beach, bringing the young stranger who would take the queen away and start a ruinous war between two kingdoms. He stood once in the roar of a battle and saw in his vision an empty moor, a huge stone rising, a naked man walking down into the dark . . .

And, sometimes, other visions, strange faint fragmentary pictures that seemed to reach him from beyond the edge of the world . . . an army of slaves building a stone mountain to be the tomb of a king . . . a beast twice the height of a horse, with a long dangling nose . . . hairy orange savages living in trees . . . a black-skinned woman who had stretched her lip till she could wrap her head in it . . . a holy man who praised his gods by lying for a whole year with one leg raised above his head . . .

True visions, but meaningless as dreams. As he drowses back into oblivion, one of them stays in his mind, changes and becomes his dream . . .

 HE strangers came to Herno behind a rattling drum, up the track from Lower Whitebone. *Brrr-snap*, went the drum, *brrr-snap*. Behind the drummer came a man walking on his hands with a demon perched in the crotch of his legs; then a dwarf with a huge head, prancing beside a big man who wore a wolf-skin over one shoulder and a spiked iron bracelet round one wrist; then two black-skinned girls wearing turbans and bright blankets, but shivering despite them in the mountain cold; then three donkey-carts, the first two carrying what looked like cages with stout wooden bars, but with their contents hidden behind draped cloths; on the third cart a tent made of tattered blue cloth with stars and symbols sewn to it—the contents were also hidden, only from time to time a huge pale hand, fingers glittering with rings, slid out from between the folds and waved or beckoned; behind the carts four women and three men, ordinary apart from their clothes, which seemed to have been botched together from garish patches; then a man walking on stilts, with difficulty because the track was steep and bad; last of all three children doing cartwheels so dizzying quick that they seemed to be bowled along by the wind, like thistledown.

Herno lay on the way from nowhere to nowhere. Its villagers saw few strangers, and were wary of those they saw. They were the last of the Old People, along with the villagers of Poum, across the mountain. They were very old. Once, long ago, their kind had filled the island, but then invaders had come out of the east, and then another wave of conquerors, and then another, each driving out the last, until the Old People were quite forgotten. Only in these two high valleys, on the way from nowhere to nowhere and on land too poor for anyone to think it worth driving them from, did the villagers keep the old ways.

But strangers did come sometimes, and four years before another procession had wound up the track, twenty-eight men wearing leather armour and iron helmets and carrying short spears—a splinter from a defeated army, lost in the mountains. They had settled on Herno like wolves, taking food and women as they wanted and murdering whoever tried to stop them, then moving on over Whitebone Pass driving twenty sheep and leaving the huts picked bare. Luckily it had been mid-summer, with most of the sheep up on the high pastures and the sparse mountain harvest not yet reaped, or Herno would have starved that winter.

That was one reason why these new travellers, who must have lost their way from somewhere to somewhere, did not get the welcome they might have expected. And perhaps they in their turn were contemptuous of the poor mountain village where they were unlikely to pass by again. At any rate they took no trouble to give pleasure and the visit did not go well.

They pitched their camp, without asking, on the Dancing Lawn, which old Angu had mown for next week's marriages. They drove holes on the soft turf and lit a fire which burnt a four-foot circle.

Then the demon which had sat between the man's legs got loose and bit little Fraio with teeth as savage as a dog's. There was no apology. Sonad caught one of their children with his hand in her apron pocket (to try that on Sonad!) and took him by the ear to be whipped by those he belonged to, but got only scowls—for herself, not the thieving child. The big man insisted on a wrestling-match with Dorin, and Dorin, huge and strong but too simple to understand what was expected of him, was suddenly picked up by the waist and slung to the ground so hard you could feel the hillside jar. He rose weeping, while the big man jeered and the dwarf cackled like a hen.

On top of all this it turned out that the strangers expected to be fed. Fed and then paid. Paid for letting Herno see what they called their marvels. Unwillingly the villagers brought out food, but as for paying . . . After a talk they decided it might be worth letting one person have a look at the marvels, so they sent Nanda with a little money, telling her to count it with care. They chose her so that she would have some gossip to exchange when she travelled back next week with her new husband to Poum—young brides often find conversation tricky with neighbours in their first few weeks, so that was a kindly thought.

Nanda came back and reported that one of the cages held an animal which the strangers said was a tiger, but it was dead. The animal in the other cage made a sort of whimpering cry, so it was alive, but the strangers had said it was too great a marvel to unveil for just one person and they would only show it if the whole village paid. The tent contained a very fat woman. The strangers expected Nanda to pay for seeing how fat she was, but Nanda, having seen, refused. The woman then said she would foretell for Nanda the man she would marry, and how rich and handsome he was going to be—two lies in one mouthful, as the saying goes—and anyway with Sonad there to see what lay beyond next week, why pay for false foretellings?

Next the strangers became angry, partly at not getting any money but more at having their marvels scorned by ignorant mountain shepherds. They swaggered among the villagers trying to pick fights, but old Angu observed that some of them seemed to have vanished, so he muttered a word or two and several of the villagers slipped away. They caught two of the children thieving in huts and the fat woman strangling hens (which she did marvellously quickly and quietly). After that the villagers rounded the whole crew up, herded them onto the Dancing Lawn and set watch on them all night.

In the morning the strangers packed and got ready to go, but before they left the fat woman stood up in her cart and spread her arms and cursed Herno in a strong deep voice like a man's. At the first words of the curse Sonad pushed forward and spread her apron between the cart and the villagers, and when the fat woman ran out of breath she gathered the apron together and shook it towards her as though she had been shaking feathers out of doors after plucking a bird. Then the strangers trailed up towards Whitebone Pass. Their drum was silent. The stilt-walker carried his poles on his shoulder. The children turned no cartwheels. The young men of Herno wanted to run ahead up sheep-tracks and roll a few small rocks down, but Sonad said no. It would not be necessary.

It was Dikki who saw what actually happened on the pass. Being Nanda's younger sister she had to find a spray of white orchises for Nanda to wear in her hair at the marriage-dances. Of course it was too soon to pick them, but since only one or two white ones might be found on a whole hillside of the mauve ones she needed to know where to find them, and so was up on the high pastures when the line of strangers snaked over the pass below.

It had been a fierce winter, freezing deep into the cliffs, veins of water swelling to ice and forcing the rocks apart, but still holding them in place until the strengthening sun thawed deep enough to melt them back to water. Perhaps the villagers should have warned the strangers, but they were still angry and eager for them to go, and in any case the rock-falls usually came in the afternoon and it was not yet mid-morning. So perhaps the fat woman's cursing had had some power in it, which Sonad had shaken back onto the strangers.

Dikki heard the cliff creak and screamed a warning, but she was too far off for the strangers to hear. There was a shushing groan as a section of cliff slid away, became boulders, and started to rumble down the slope.

Now the strangers heard. Dikki saw the white dots of their turned faces. The big man picked up the dwarf and ran with him. The fat woman tumbled out of her tent and waddled. The others scampered. The donkey-drivers lashed at their animals. The front donkey panicked and tried to turn upwards off the track, blocking the path behind. The drivers left the carts and ran.

In fact the strangers had been lucky. The falling rocks came from the southernmost end of the cliff, so they were already almost past the danger-point and most of the fall went thundering down the slope behind them. Only one boulder the size of a man's head must have hit an outcrop twenty paces above the path. It glanced off, hurtling through the air straight at the middle cart, and struck the cage on its top edge.

There was a crack. The cart tilted. The donkey struggled to hold its footing, slipped and fell. The cage tilted gently out of the cart and, landing on its damaged edge, fell apart.

The strangers shouted and began to run back, in spite of the danger from lesser stones which were still rattling down, but before they reached the cart a brown thing struggled out of the wreckage and stood up. Dikki, who had keen eyes, said it looked something like the demon which had bitten Fraio, but larger. And it had only one leg.

The nearest donkey-driver rushed at it, arms spread wide for a grab, but it leaped out of reach like a grasshopper down the slope. Another leap, and another, and then a fold of ground hid it from Dikki. The strangers ran streaming down the hill in chase. Though she saw the creature only for those few instants, she was quite certain about the single leg, and said too that there was something wrong with its foot, which was wound round and round with bandages so that it seemed swollen like a great mushroom. Despite that, it could still leap like a grasshopper.

Dikki ran back to Herno to tell what she had seen, and the men came out with their bear-clubs and slings. They found the strangers spread out along the low pastures, hunting for the thing, and told them to go away. The strangers refused until some of the men took practice shots at suitable targets to show what they could do. In the end the strangers left, raging.

Next week the excitement of the marriages took over. Turf was cut from a meadow to replace the burnt circle, and the holes were filled. If the villagers from Poum noticed the scars they were too polite to mention them. Nanda danced delightfully and the two brides from Poum almost as well. The adventure with the strangers was discussed, but the brown leaping thing that came out of the cage did not seem an important part of it.

Later in the year the thing was seen on the mountain-sides, always far off. It was very shy. The children tried to stalk it but got nowhere near. It did no harm. Summer went by with no alarms, but summer was short in the mountains, almost too short for all the jobs that had to be done if Herno was to come safe through next winter, and it seemed little time after the marriages before the first snows fell and Whitebone Pass was blocked once more.

At first no one recognised the thing's footprints on the snowfields for what they were. A hunter going to check his snares would find the cord loosed from the hare's neck with the body lying beside it and close by a rounded hollow in the snow three handbreadths wide and more than twice that long. If the hare had been stolen it would not be by the brown thing —there would be a fox's prints to prove that. Sometimes the hunters might find the imprint of a human hand, small as a child's. Later, when they had learnt to recognise the hollows, they began to find them out on open slopes with no other mark near. Only by studying the signs carefully—the broken edges of the rim, the scatterings of loose snow round it—a clever tracker could see that the marks had been made by something large and soft landing in the snow from one direction and immediately bouncing on. Knowing that, he could follow the marks across the slope, some ten or fifteen good paces apart.

Until winter hardened these marks stayed far from the village, but then they came closer. Dogs would bark. In the stillness of the dark a woman lying awake might hear a whimpering cry, faint but near. Next morning she would see the strange tracks, the marks closer than before, as though the creature's leaps were getting shorter. It would have been easy now to track the thing to wherever it laired, but no one had the time.

A week before the fire-games Sonad sent for Dikki, who was her niece.

"I had a dream," she said. "Take Dorin with you. Go up the gulley the far side of Bikarhead and see what you can find."

So the two put on their snow-shoes and set out. Dorin carried Dikki most of the way, not because she needed the help but because he liked to carry and touch. They found the tracks crossing the steep wild slope below Bikarhead, each mark so close to the next that they sometimes overlapped, and just above them all the way small handprints, showing that the thing could no longer move upright. The creature itself was lying half-buried in a drift in the gulley, apparently dead. Dorin carried it back to Sodan's hut with Dikki shoeing behind.

It had a human face and body with dark brown skin, smooth as a child's except for frost-chapping. The closed eyelids were large and long-lashed but the mouth and nose very small. The hair was silky, blue-black. The body was wrapped round with a thick brown woollen cloak. There was only one leg. Though the body was no bigger than Dikki's the leg was as thick as a big man's. The foot was so covered with wrappings that its size and shape could not be guessed.

Sonad took wood she had been saving for the fire-games and built up the fire, then laid the creature beside it, just so close as not to burn. Twice she turned it round. Suddenly the creature coughed. Dikki had some warmed milk ready and tried to dribble it into the tiny mouth, but the lips clamped firm against her. Sonad took the little brown body in her arms, cradling it so that Dikki could try again, but as she did so the creature opened its eyes.

It stared at the blazing logs.

"Aaaahh," it sighed. "Aaaahh."

It wriggled, not to get away from Sonad's embrace nor to stretch its hands as a child might have done towards the fire, but to move its great foot closer. At once the bandages started to scorch, filling the hut with a prickly heat, but as soon as Sonad tried to pull it away the creature whimpered like a hurt cat. Though it must now have felt the burning it still did not withdraw its foot, but struggled to a sitting position and then leaned forward and with trembling little hands unlashed the bandages. There were not nearly as many of them as there had seemed to be. All the bulk of the bundle was made of what it held, a single enormous foot.

The foot had ten toes.

While Dikki raked the smouldering wrappings aside the creature spread that great foot in front of the fire. It opened up like a flower until it was almost as broad as it was long. The light of the flames came through it so that Dikki could see the fan of fine bones spreading out and up from the heel, and the network of veins between them. At the top the ten toes waved gently, like weed in the pool of a stream. The two great toes were at the centre and the little ones at the outside.

All this while the creature seemed not to know what was happening to it, or where it was. It had acted as an animal does, without thinking, because that is its nature. It may have been in what mountain people call the snow-dream, that strange comfortable daze of warmth and home-coming which overtakes a man who has lost his way among the peaks and then become too weak with cold to struggle further. As his eyes close for the last time he dreams the snow-dream.

Suddenly the creature seemed to wake and see where it was. It jerked its head this way and that, staring at Dorin, then Dikki, then up into Sonad's face. They smiled, and Sonad made the clucking sound a mother uses to comfort a frightened child, though she herself had no children—that was the price of her gift of foretelling. The creature stared huge-eyed into the dark parts of the hut. It narrowed its foot, shrinking it in from the edges, then with a quick movement stood on its single leg.

"Open the door, Dorin," said Sonad.

The moment it saw daylight the creature gathered its foot-wrappings and leaped to the threshold. It stood poised for the next leap, black and strange against the snow-glare. One of the quick hill blizzards was starting. The flakes whipped past. The bitter air whined in the eaves. The creature looked back into the hut where the flames still wavered above the red embers. Sonad and Dikki moved away, leaving a clear space round the hearth. In three wary hops, looking back over its shoulder each time towards the whistling blizzard, the creature came back into the hut and spread its foot by the fire. Dorin closed the door.

"Not *it*," said Dikki. "*She.*"

"Then she must have a name," said old Angu. "Even dogs have names."

"I'll ask her," said Dikki.

But the creature's name seemed to be a string of bubbles and gurgles, such as a baby makes when it is pretending to talk. No one could pronounce them, and nor could the creature say the villagers' names. She tried. She called Dorin Gollill and Dikki Yingi, so they called her Lall, which was a sound they thought everyone could make, though it turned out not enough to please Lall, who always referred to herself as at least Lallalallalall, and often three times that.

She was a marvel all right. At least the strangers had not lied about that. Nobody, after being with her for half an hour or so, could have doubted she was human. She was shy of meeting anyone new, but with Herno snowbound there were soon none of those. She needed to be introduced by someone she trusted, with names properly spoken and touching of palms. But once through the shyness she was very quick and clever. Though she could herself say very few words she soon understood everything that was said, and picked up the way things were done and helped like a

daughter in Sonad's hut. She was very little cost to keep as she ate so little
—nothing with meat in it—and drank only water. Her one fault was that
she was always trying to sneak another log onto the fire.

In fact she seemed to live on heat, to feed on it. On clear days, however
cold the air, she would find a sheltered place and lie on her back and spread
her foot towards the sun, so that it seemed like a great pale flower moving
slowly on its stalk, following the path of the sun, as a sun-daisy does. After
days like this she was especially bright and cheerful, her black eyes sparkling
and her little mouth drawing itself into an O to smile. Or she would rise
from her back and leap among the huts for pleasure. She could, if she
chose, jump clean over a hut. In fact, soon after she came to Herno there
was a particularly vicious storm which stripped tiles from roofs all over
the village, and Lall saved a lot of awkward ladder-work by simply hopping
up and fixing the tiles back. Her big soft foot spread her small weight
around so that she broke nothing, and she seemed able to shape it to the
surface so that she sucked herself onto the steepest pitches and clung there,
as a fly does. Strangely she did not seem to feel the cold, delicate and tender
though the foot looked when spread in front of a fire. Bunched it became
tough and leathery—well-tanned leather, both supple and strong.

So, marvel though she was, by winter's end the villagers had become
used to her and stopped marvelling. She was one of themselves, ordinary.

A few days after the snows cleared from Lower Whitebone, long before
Whitebone Pass itself would be free, Sonad woke in the night. Her husband,
Alpet, snorted and turned in his sleep, but Sonad got softly out of bed.
Lall, in her cot on the other side of the hearth, had woken at her stirring.

"Go and find Dorin," said Sonad.

Lall hopped away. Sonad gathered a satchel of food, wrapped blankets
round it and tied them into a bundle. When Lall came back with Dorin,
sleepy but smiling through his yawns, Sonad tied the bundle across his
shoulders, then picked Lall up and put her in his arms.

"Take her up to the cave below Bikarhead," she said. "Carry her all the
way."

Happy to be told to do what he would have done anyway Dorin shambled
off into the night. Sonad did not go back to bed. First she took Lall's cot
apart and stored the pieces among the rafters, then sprinkled and swept
the place where it had been. She swept every inch of the hut. She put away
Lall's cup and spoon and dish, so that there were only two of each on the
shelf. She hid in the rafters the cushion on which Lall sat when she warmed
her foot at the fire. Dawn found her sweeping round the outside of the hut,
and as they woke she set her neighbours sweeping too.

They did not put their brooms away till the sun was high. A little later
the strangers came up the track from Lower Whitebone.

139

This time they rattled no drum, perhaps because they wanted to come without warning, but more likely their drummer had left them. They were only five—the big man and the dwarf, the fat woman in her tent on the one cart, one child leading the donkey and another slouching by its wheel. The donkey was skin and bone, the big man's skin was dull, the dwarf whined, the children turned no cartwheels. You did not need hawk's eyes to see that they had had a bad winter. The other change from their former coming was that this time the big man held the leash of a hound, which snuffled all the time at the ground.

They asked to be fed and produced money, coins the size of wheat-seed, but money all the same. They talked in quiet voices and smiled too much. Everyone watched the children every instant, but no lean little hand strayed near anyone's pocket. The fat woman called Sonad "sister" and showed her a mystery with coloured cards. Meanwhile the big man strolled through the village with the snuffling hound. Sometimes he held a brown rag under its nose. He studied every patch of soft or dusty ground, and at last came back glum to the Dancing Lawn and spoke to old Angu.

"Last year we lost one of my animals on the mountain-side."

"A brown thing?" said Angu.

"You've seen it?"

"One of the children said she saw a brown thing," said Angu, who preferred not to tell lies, even to liars. "When the rocks hit your cart it went away down over the lower pastures. Our young men found you there."

The big man must have had a hide like a bear not to feel the rebuke.

"This animal is mine," he said in a loud voice. "It is valuable to me, but not to anyone else. You cannot eat it or make use of it. Whoever brings it to me alive I will pay him ten gold coins. If anyone finds its body as the snows melt, let him put it in vinegar and pickle it and bring it to me and I will pay him two gold coins. I will pay one gold coin for the foot alone. One gold coin. Two gold coins. Ten gold coins."

Ragged though he was he felt between the inner and outer leather of his wide belt and drew out the coins. He held them up for everyone to see. In Herno one gold coin would have bought five huts and their contents.

"Has anyone seen an animal belonging to this man?" called Angu.

The villagers shook their heads, looking the big man straight in the eye. They had no bad consciences about this. Lall was not an animal. She did not belong to anyone.

The big man took the dog and quartered the nearer slopes but found no trail. The strangers marched off before nightfall, but Sonad did not send Dikki to fetch Dorin for three more days.

140

Having had this warning they decided not to take Lall over the hill to Poum for that year's marriages. Poum was on a slightly more frequented track, along which two or three parties of strangers might come in a summer. But when Sonad told Lall she wept and whimpered so that they changed their minds. There was no bride from Herno that year, but the unmarried girls practised the dances so that they would be skilful when their turn came, and do the village credit. Naturally Lall, being Dikki's friend, practised with them, inventing steps of her own to replace the two-legged skippings, using the opposite sides of her foot as though they were almost separate, so that if she had been wearing the long skirt of a bride you could hardly have told. And of course, when it came to the leaps through the flower-ropes . . . !

Dikki went over the mountain to ask Nanda to explain to the Poum people that a stranger had come to live with them, rather odd-looking, but one of themselves now. Sonad sewed Lall a skirt longer and fuller than the other girls would wear, to hide the great foot, and Lall discovered a way of moving without hops by rippling the sole in much the way a caterpillar ripples its body. She could only move slowly, but glided solemnly along while her friends giggled.

Sonad made no attempt to hide her dark skin. It was not the custom between the two villages to ask or explain very much, but at the same time they felt it was wrong to deceive each other. Indeed, but for the fright they had had from the strangers, they would probably have let Poum see Lall's oddity and left it to their good manners how to behave.

The weddings went well. It was a pity there were no brides from Herno, but the two from Poum sufficed. (There had to be at least two. A single marriage was unthinkable. When that possibility arose they put it off till next year but met as usual and sat around the Dancing Lawn and played their bagpipes and sang the old choruses and got drunk together.) The Poum people were perfectly friendly with Lall, though finding she could not speak they assumed she was simple-minded, like Dorin. Anyway, she enjoyed herself, and watched the dance of the brides with especial delight. It was always a pretty sight.

That summer passed and winter came and nothing unusual happened, and the same for two more winters, in the first of which old Angu died, so Alpet became old Alpet and spoke for the village. He was not so wise as Angu, people felt, but with Sonad to foretell for him he would manage. Then, late in the third winter, Sonad, sitting by the hearth one evening with Alpet across from her and Lall on her cushion between them, looked up from her lacework and said, "I have just seen. I shall die this summer, nine days after the weddings."

Alpet gaped. For a moment it looked as though he might die then and there, with the shock of it, but then he snorted and said, "You have seen stupidity. There will be no weddings this summer. Poum have no brides, and from Herno there is only Dikki."

"I will see Dikki leap through the flower-ropes before I die," said Sonad.

"Then you have a year, and more than a year. Perhaps by then you will have seen something more sensible."

Sonad stared in front of her, looking at nothing in the room.

"I will see Lall's marriage-dance too," she said.

"Lall! We cannot ask any of the Poum men . . ."

Lall put up her small brown hand and touched Sonad's arm.

"Gollill," she said.

Alpet snorted again. Then he thought for a little and said, "Dorin ought to have a wife, and again we cannot ask any of the Poum girls . . ."

So it was arranged. The Poum people may have thought it a little odd, but they were glad to be spared the embarrassment of refusing to find bride or groom for the two Herno simpletons, and glad too that there would be proper dances that summer.

Which indeed there were. Never had a bride danced like Lall. She wore white orchises in her hair, which Fraio had found for her, and the right long dress, though she was no taller than she had been when she first came to Herno. The Poum people had prepared their faces for kindly tolerance, but when they saw Lall skimming over the flower-ropes their smiles changed. And when they saw the great pale ten-toed foot beneath the billowing cloth (for by then Lall had completely forgotten caution in her excitement and was leaping high over everyone's heads) they changed again. The Herno people looked at Sonad, lying on her litter and watching the dance with the big eyes of the dying. Perhaps she should have signalled to Lall to dance less wildly, or perhaps by then it was already too late, and Herno should have told Poum all about Lall from the very beginning . . .

Sonad died as she had seen, nine days after the dances. She lay as she had done so often those last pain-filled months, with Lall kneeling by her side, the small dark hands folded into the coarse old grey ones, and Sonad whispering what she knew. Lall kissed her and went back to the hut she was helping Dorin build, and Alpet sat with Sonad so that they could say the good-byes. Then she died.

Nobody had imagined Dorin would ever build a hut. He simply would not get it to stand. Things did not piece themselves together in his mind in a way that would let him see how to drive two uprights into the ground and lay a beam across them to hold them together so that they could take the outward thrust of the rafters. But Lall, without words, seemed able to make his mind do the piecing, and he built her a hut, small and crooked but sound enough. Everyone in the village brought them the doorway presents on the morning Dorin put the lintel in, so that they were furnished like any other new-wed couple.

Of course they did not seem quite like other couples, but not for the reason you might have thought. In Herno you married a bride or groom from Poum according to whose turn it was—there was seldom much question of choosing. Then you learnt to love each other over the years, if you were lucky. Herno was not used to lovers, and that is what Lall and Dorin were. They filled the air around them with their happiness in each other. They were never apart. Dorin of course wanted to carry Lall wherever they went, while Lall wanted to leap all round him, so they invented a game together, Lall leaping from twenty yards away into his arms and he catching her like a flying ball and hugging her to him and then tossing her free (somehow she always landed on her foot) and she bouncing back into his arms again. You would see them coming across the pastures in the evening, playing their game, and whatever your troubles at the moment you could not help sharing their happiness, and smiling for them.

The only thing that troubled anyone was that Lall refused to cook meat, so Dorin had to do with vegetables. He did not seem to mind, and there was little harm in summer, but it would be hard, people thought, to get a man through the snows with no meat in his meals. That seemed all there was to worry about until one morning, just before harvest, when the big man strode up the track. This time he came with soldiers.

He was older. There was grey in his beard, and the scar of some fight down his cheek, but he wore a new wolfskin and his skin shone with good feeding. He gave orders to the soldiers, keeping two for his escort and sending the rest on up the track towards Whitebone Pass, then swaggered across to where old Alpet sat by the Dancing Lawn.

"Where is the other old fool?" he said.

"Angu is dead," said Alpet.

"And you are the old fool who has taken his place?"

"I speak for Herno."

"You will do, then. I speak to Herno."

The big man opened his belt and counted out ten gold coins, which he tossed one by one at Alpet's feet.

"Now you will give me back my Sciopod," he said.

"Sciopod?"

"The brown thing the child saw, as the other old fool said. He lied to me. You all lied to me. But I have forgiven you and I will keep my word. I will give you ten gold coins for my Sciopod."

"Nobody lied to you," said Alpet. "A human being is not an animal. A human being belongs to no one."

The big man laughed and flashed his white teeth round at the villagers, who by now had gathered to listen.

"You are fools," he said. "I have made my living from people like you, so I am kindly disposed to fools. Listen. I now serve a powerful lord, master of nine strong castles and many miles of land. It is my duty to amuse him with new things. One night I told him the story of my Sciopod, and he was greatly pleased. He is not easy to please—remember that, fools. Now, there was a traveller among the company, a seller of turquoise, who had come to my master's castle passing through these very mountains, and had heard gossip of a creature that had danced at some peasant merry-making this spring. The merchant thought it all a fable, but I questioned him closely and from the description he was given I know that the creature he was told about can only have been my Sciopod. My master, learning that it was still alive, has expressed a wish to see it. So, now, give me my Sciopod."

The villagers could not meet his gaze, but they did not know where Lall was, nor Dorin. When they had woken that morning the door of the crooked little hut had hung open. Blankets were gone and the food-jars empty. Sonad, of course, had told Lall what she knew, but since then Lall had done no foretellings, having no language to tell with. Still, she had woken in the night and gone, taking Dorin with her.

"A human being belongs to no one," mumbled Alpet.

"I am hungry with this mountain air," said the big man, "so now I will go and have my meal. You will have that time to think. I will leave the money here to help you."

He poked the coins with his sandal. Dew from the grass made them glitter in the mountain sunlight.

"I have soldiers stopping the passes, top and bottom," said the big man. "You cannot run away. When I come back from my meal I will bring some of them. If you give me my Sciopod, you will keep my money and I will go away. If not, I will tell my soldiers to question you, every one of you, man, woman and child, using what methods amuse them. Since you have stolen my Sciopod, which is worth a hundred villages, I will take your sheep and your possessions in exchange. I will burn your crops and your huts, to teach you not to steal again. I will take the clothes from your backs and leave you naked. You may think you can run away and hide on the mountain. In that case I will leave the valley stoppered and go and tell my master how you have thwarted his wish. My master enjoys hunting, and has good hounds and trackers. That is all. You have my meal-time to make up your minds. Fools though you are, you will not find it difficult."

144

He scuffed his foot against the coins so that they clinked together and strode away, leaving the villagers to their decision. It was not a hard choice. Lall was not there to give back, but if she had been none of them would have touched her or held her to prevent her from leaping away. Perhaps they were frightened enough to have stood aside and let the big man take her if he could, but as for giving, she was not theirs to give.

The big man walked with his escort down towards Lower Whitebone, where he had left his cook with the rest of the soldiers to prepare his meal. He was pleased with himself. He had felt the villagers' fear and dismay and was sure that they would now do what he wanted. He had not lied to them much, apart from what would happen when they had handed Lall over and he had her safe in her new cage. He was considering the details of his revenge on Herno when Lall met him at the mouth of Lower Whitebone, where the cliff ran straight up above and straight down to the muttering snow-fed river below, with the track on a ledge between.

He stopped for a moment, stared and then walked forward, grinning. She gave two small leaps, only a few paces each, backwards into the narrows of the track. The big man spoke over his shoulder to his escort to stand at intervals behind him, so that if Lall tried to leap over his head they would be there to catch her. He hallooed to the soldiers at the other end of the narrows to spread themselves out in the same way, then stole towards her like a stalking cat with his huge hands poised, ready to clutch. Lall waited with her head drawn back and her ten toes fluttering in the dust of the track. It being high summer she wore no wrappings.

Just before he reached her, just as his trained quick muscles flexed to grab, she leaped.

Out, away, over the cliff edge, a tremendous spring, then falling, tumbling over and over, her brown foot shaped like an autumn leaf, dwindling towards the black rocks and the green-and-white water.

The big man watched her fall, craning, mouth open, hands spread wide, still poised in the clutch that had never closed. He did not see Dorin coming.

Dorin rushed out of his hiding-place back beside the road, slapping the two soldiers aside as he charged between them. His mouth was drawn down in a silent howl and his cheeks glistened with weeping. He seized the big man by the waist, lifted him bodily and leaped out and away. They did not reach the river, as Lall had, but fell somewhere among the scrawny trees which clung to a footing in the rockfall at the bottom of the cliff.

Back in the village the men waited with slings and bear-clubs. The women and children had gone up Bikarhead with all the food they could carry. When the big man did not return Alpet sent Duni to explore. He found the soldiers at the mouth of Lower Whitebone, still peering over the cliff and arguing in loud voices what to do, and learnt from the argument that the big man must have fallen over. So he went back to Herno and reported.

Alpet picked up the ten gold coins from where they lay untouched in the grass of the Dancing Lawn and took the men down to Lower Whitebone, where he found the soldiers still at odds over what to do. From them he learnt what had happened to Lall and Dorin and the big man. He sent Ponda to Whitebone Pass to tell those soldiers they could come back, then started to bargain with the ones already there. There were not so many as the big man had implied, and they were leaderless, whereas the villagers, though worse armed, were filled with anger and determination after Lall and Dorin's death. In the end the soldiers accepted three gold coins as the price of going away.

By now it was almost dusk. Alpet took the other seven coins and tossed them, one by one, over the cliff. Then he sent Duni up to Bikarhead to tell the women it was safe to come back. They spent the evening re-arranging the jobs that everyone would do next day. A whole day had been wasted by the big man coming, and there was never any time to spare in summer if Herno was to get through the winter without freezing or starving.

Winter rules the moor. Snow drifts deep against rock. Pale sun softens the drift until drips runnel on stone. Night brings frost, starching snow hard, binding water to ice. In a crack of one rock a freak of this thawing and freezing forms two ice lips, a whistling mouth. In the night breeze it blows a gently throbbing note, but when the gale rises it begins to shriek, shrill and loud enough to pierce through earth and rock to the slot of dark where he lies. He wakes and listens to the sound. He feels the whole deadness of midwinter.

Woman's time. The Powers take many shapes in the tribes' minds. Ages beyond ages before, the Powers had been female, breeders of life, bearers of milk, mysterious bringers of seed to ripeness. Then, somehow, they had seemed to change. In the tribes' minds these she-Powers had borne sons, young male gods, strong and greedy, begetters and slayers, who had seized the sunlight and the summer, driving the older she-Powers into hiding, into the dark of the moon, into the dead of winter. But there they kept their strength. Then there were rituals only women could take part in, secrets only women could be told. Then men were afraid.

There had been a boy who watched the ravens. There was a man who slept under rock. Between that starting and this ending he had walked many paths, he had been the wolf in the forest, the salmon in the flood, the raven on the cliff. He had been the woman at the hearth also. For seven years he had worn woman's dress, spoken woman's speech, cooked with his left hand, slept in the bed of a fighter. It had been no punishment and no shame, but rich years giving knowledge and power. He had walked with the Three Queens of Death and not been afraid.

Why should he? Their terror was never in them. It was in the minds of the men who had made them so.

Now, at the heart of woman's time, he can make the wind-shriek his lullaby and give himself peacefully back to his mother dark.

ENCHANTRESS

HE turrets of her castle rose above tree-tops, always with cloud somewhere around them. On storm-days you could not see them at all, but even in clearest summer scarfs of mist twisted through them, so that you could never be sure of the whole outline, or be able to swear that they were exactly the same as they had been yesterday.

Around the castle lay a wood, not large but very dense, enormous hoary trees dangling with mosses and creepers. The underwoods were immense arching brambles with thorns as long as a man's thumb, blood-red and razor-sharp. In among the brambles lived thin green serpents with golden eyes. Huge rooks nested in the tree-tops, and small bats under the turret roofs. By day and night these black creatures would wing silently over the fields, and perch to spy and listen, and then fly back with the news of each farm—which wife had cursed her husband, which father had hit his daughter, which child had lied to her mother. *She* liked to know such things.

That is what they called her—*She*. *She*, with a dropping of the voice but a lingering weight on the word. Nobody knew her name. *She* took care of that. But *She* knew every name in all that country. When a baby was christened there would always be a bat hanging in the rafters of the church or a rook perched at the window to learn the new child's name. The worst thing you could do was to try to keep the name secret by whispering it to the priest and having him whisper it over the child, for if you did that then your crops would wither in your fields and your cattle sicken and white worms breed and gnaw in your rafters until your roof fell in. Otherwise that was good land with a fine climate, bringing rich harvests, because *She* kept it so. It was better for her to know your baby's name than for your whole family to starve. But *She* did not seem to mind if you made the new child's name long and difficult, in the hope that her black messenger would not remember.

There was another custom at christenings which might have seemed odd to strangers. All the guests, as they inspected the baby, would take the utmost trouble to speak ill of it. "Ugly little shrew," they would say, and the mother would loudly agree. "Doesn't look like that one will live long," they would say, "—nasty temper, though." And the father would bellow that all his children were an ache to the eyesight but this was the worst of the lot.

There was a reason for this ill-saying. If *She* were to be told of a handsome child, then the day would come . . .

It was a foolish custom still. The rooks and the bats knew what to look for and saw the child day by day. It could not be helped that some of the children grew beautiful, and then, when they were about fourteen, those

151

ones would be drawn towards the castle. No use locking them up or watching them night and day or sending them to far-off farms, because there would always come a moment when the locks failed to snap or the watcher drowsed or the miles somehow folded in on themselves, and then the child would wander down to the wood's edge and vanish. The only compensation was that when a child was lost in this way the farm from which it came would grow wonderful crops that year.

In one particular village, close to the castle woods, two babies happened to be born on the same day, and in the same minute of that day. The girl was the most beautiful infant anybody could remember seeing, and the boy was utterly hideous. He was born with coarse black hair, protruding ears, a huge mouth and a ridiculous squashed nose, but the worst thing of all was his squint. Many babies squint at first, but it was clear this child would never look two-eyed at anything, and what's more his left eye was a bright and piercing blue while his right eye was soft brown. Everything anyone could say against him at his christening was true, whereas the girl had such striking dark blue eyes and golden curls and pearly-rosy skin that even the crabbiest old cousins forgot their manners and called her lovely. The parents did their best to confuse the rook on the window by naming her Farabinellabinillabefarrabellilla. There was no point in fretting about the boy, so he was christened Dan.

No other children had been born in that village for two years and none were born for three more, so Fara (which is what she was called for everyday) and Dan grew up together and played with each other and walked and talked and adventured together in the small adventures of children. Fara became more beautiful every year, but Dan's looks did not improve at all. He was so ugly that people were afraid of him. Especially they did not care for the way he looked at them—either way, this is, for when he gazed at them with his bright blue eye he seemed to pierce right through to the centre of their being and see exactly what they were, and when he stared at them with his soft brown eye he seemed to be seeing something else, what they might have been, perhaps, or what they ought to be, or what they could never be. Eyes, people felt, should see the surface and nothing else. Only Fara did not mind his looks, either way. Perhaps she was used to him, or perhaps he saw her the same with both eyes.

Of course Fara was forbidden from the first to go near the woods. Her parents considered selling their farm and moving to somewhere at the furthest edge of the country, but the land would not be so good there. The closer you farmed to the castle the better your harvests, and since Fara had been born crops had been wonderful on her parents' farm, whereas at Dan's they had been scant and diseased and it had been a struggle to get by. Nobody thought this strange. *She* would be pleased with Fara's parents

152

for having such a beautiful child to send to her, but she would certainly punish Dan's for bringing such a hideous creature into her country.

Nobody told Dan to keep clear of the woods—what was the point? Long before he was old enough to understand what would probably happen to Fara he was fascinated by them. He would loiter along the edges peering at everything with his bright blue eye and making small experiments. He learnt that his father's best hatchet would not cut the brambles, and that the green snakes spat a poison which burnt his skin like fire. He trapped birds and set them free under the branches, and observed that they never flew into the shelter of the trees but always out into the perilous open air.

At other times he lay further off and gazed with his dreamy brown eye at the shadows among the trees and the turrets rising above, and the shifting drifting clouds. It is hard to say what he learnt by doing this, but no doubt something.

After twelve years of bumper crops Fara's parents were rich enough to build a special house for their daughter, a squat tower with thick stone walls, one room below and one above, no windows on the ground floor, and those upstairs small and barred and facing away from the wood. The smith forged an iron girdle for Fara, and a chain, and a strong iron shackle to be bolted into the floor of the upstairs room. The door was a foot thick, oak, with two locks with different keys, one for her father and one for her mother. On her thirteenth birthday they took her in and chained her fast.

They decided too that from now on they would trust only themselves, in case her beauty persuaded somebody to set her free, but they allowed her friends one last visit to say good-bye. As he kissed her Dan whispered in her ear.

"When you go, take me."

It was midsummer, with a full moon, when seven green snakes slid out at midnight from the wood. They slithered up the wall of Fara's tower and dribbled their poison on the iron bars, which melted away. They glided down into the room and dribbled again on the links at either end of Fara's chain. Wide awake, she rose from her bed, climbed to the window and hooked the end of the chain over the stub of one of the melted bars. Silently she let herself down.

Like a pale angel in her nightdress she glided down the village street towards the wood, towards the turrets sparkling above the treetops in the moonlight. Then she stopped.

The snakes hissed, but she drew her elbows to her sides and clenched her fists so that her nails bit into her palms. With shudders and spasms she forced herself to turn aside, up the little alley towards the house where Dan lived. Every step was a struggle, like a shepherd forcing himself through a blizzard to look for snow-smothered sheep. When she reached Dan's window she knocked three times with her clenched fist on the shutter, but then the witch-trance took her and she was gliding back down the alley, down the street, between the rich fields towards the wood.

Dan caught her as she walked in under the shadow of the trees. He did not try to stop her, but put his arm round her waist and she put hers round his. They drew each other close and walked into the dark.

No moon could pierce those layers of leaves, but just as the children reached the first trees a line of light glowed, the colour of moonbeams, and in it the brambles arched aside and the creepers coiled themselves up, leaving a clear path paved with stone. Sweet high music began, voices like birds and bells. "Farabinellabinillabefarrabellilla," they sang. "Welcome, oh welcome, Farabinellabinillabefarrabellilla."

As they walked through the growing arch the brambles trembled and heaved, straining in towards Dan to try and bar his path. Savage branchlets lashed at his face, but Fara put up her free hand to shield him and they glanced aside. Green snakes crowded hissing at the edge of the path, but they could not spit their poison at Dan with Fara walking so close in the filmy stuff of her nightdress. Though there was no wind the trees creaked, as if straining in a gale. The voices faltered in their song. "Farabinilla . . . Farabella . . . Faranilla . . ."

The path ended at a bone-white bridge over a black moat. Guarding the bridge stood a centaur. As soon as it saw Dan the marvellous creature reared on its hind legs and gave a shout which was half the neigh of a war-horse and half the battle-cry of a warrior. With a roaring snort it charged, whirling an iron-bound club in its human hands.

Dan stared at it with his bright blue eye.

"How do you eat grass?" he said.

The centaur stopped.

"What is that to you?" it roared.

"You must eat grass to feed your horse-part, but I cannot see how you chew it with human teeth and swallow it down a human throat. You cannot ever eat enough, so your horse-part must starve."

The centaur lowered its club and shook its head dazedly from side to side. Suddenly its glossy flanks caved in. Gaunt ribs ridged its staring hide and the big bones of its hind-quarters jutted up like rocks on a hilltop.

"Let me pass and I will tell you the answer," said Dan.

The centaur staggered aside and let the children onto the bridge. Dan

turned and gazed at the centaur with his soft brown eye.

"You do not starve because I suppose you not to," he said.

As he spoke the centaur's hide grew glossy and its muscles swelled back into place. It picked up its club and swung it in a thoughtful manner as it went back to its post.

When Fara and Dan reached the crown of the bridge three mermaids surfaced in the moat below and opened their mouths to sing the magic song which draws men to them, to dive into the water, to follow them down, swimming deeper and deeper, to drown in their arms.

Dan looked at the mermaids with his bright blue eye.

"Do you have gills?" he said.

The mermaids' mouths stayed open but their song did not come.

"If you do not have gills you cannot breathe under water," said Dan. "You must drown too."

At those words the mermaids changed. Scales rippled up over the ivory skin of their bodies, spiky fins rose from their spines and their arms began to melt into their sides. In a moment they would have been three large round-mouthed fishes, but Dan looked at them with his brown eye and spoke again.

"You can breathe under water because I suppose you can," he said.

The spines sank back; the skin became soft, glistening like mother-of-pearl; the mermaids grew long slender arms, which they waved in thanks before they sank back under the water. Fara and Dan, still clutching each other close, walked down off the bridge.

The castle had a huge arched gateway, whose doors stood open wide, but as they approached it the door on Dan's side slammed shut and the other swung in, leaving a slot just wide enough for one person. The children did not hesitate. They walked so that Dan was aiming at the opening and Fara at the black, iron-studded timber of the door itself. It seemed immovable but she did not flinch, and just before she walked straight into it it swung groaningly aside to let her through.

They heard a wild baying, and out of a kennel just inside the gate rushed a black hound, three-headed, with three sets of fangs drawn wide to tear and rip. Dan stared at it with his bright blue eye.

"Which head controls which leg?" he said.

The hound halted. The three heads looked at each other. A hind leg twitched up to scratch an ear, to help that head think, but the other two heads were not ready for the movement so the hound toppled over and lay there with its legs waving in the air, like a beetle on its back.

Dan let go of Fara for a moment and heaved the creature onto its feet, where he held it steady while Fara scratched two of its heads and he scratched the third with his free hand. He gazed at it with his dreamy brown eye.

"You stand because I suppose you to," he said.

The hound went back to its kennel, cocking its heads from side to side as though thinking the matter out under its three thick skulls. Fara and Dan held each other close again and walked side by side across a courtyard and up a marble stair to a tall black archway. This time the doors did not try to stop Dan.

When they came out of the moonlight all seemed dark. Only, far off, was a single prick of yellow light. They walked across a vast shadowy hall towards it, and as they came nearer they saw it was the flame of a large candle, standing on a table that held an enormous book. Sitting behind the table, reading the book, was a little old man dressed all in black.

The old man looked up at the children's footfall and peered at them over his spectacles. His bleary eyes brightened at the sight of Fara. He put his nose back into the book and read her name aloud, speaking it syllable by syllable as his finger traced it across the page.

"Farabinellabinillabefarrabellilla . . . Yes, yes, indeed you are chosen. Pass through, my dear. The Queen is waiting . . .

"But now, as for you, young man, hum, hum . . . oh dear me . . . what have we here? . . . tsk . . . how unfortunate! Do you know, I actually remember the event—such a beautiful long name for the girl-child—and very proper, too, if I may say so, my dear . . . where was I? Oh yes, I had to dip my quill again to finish it and I let too much ink . . . tsk, careless, careless."

The children came a pace closer and could see what he was peering at in the big book. Immediately above Fara's name was a black blob, roughly the shape of a frog. It was just large enough to cover three letters.

The old man looked up with a sigh and peered at Dan.

"Still, it hardly matters," he said. "Even my poor old eyes can see that you are certainly *not* one of those chosen."

"You don't know my name?" said Dan.

"As it happens, thoroughly unfortunate, hum, hum . . ."

"Then you can't stop me."

"Well, of course, those are the regulations, but as I say it is perfectly obvious . . ."

The children left him mumbling and walked round the table to the door beyond. It was shut, but opened at Fara's touch, and they went through.

Inside was a huge room, lit bright as day. It glowed with colour from banners and tapestries and jewel-bright birds perched in golden cages. A soft crimson carpet led up the centre of the room to a platform with a throne of ebony and ivory, and there *She* waited.

Or did she?

She was difficult to see properly, even for Dan with his two ways of seeing. When he looked at her with his brown eye she kept changing. She was fair-haired, with blue eyes and creamy skin, almost the image of what Fara would become when she was older . . . but now she was brown as timber and her hair as black as the feather of a rook, and her eyes darker still . . . now pale as bone, seeming to have no blood anywhere except in her crimson lips . . . now ruddy and strong, with emerald eyes and flowing coppery hair . . . and always young, the same woman through the changes, beautiful, old as the world . . .

While Dan's brown eye stared at the shape-shifting queen his blue eye had to look past her, and it saw something else, not the rich room with its candles and bright colours, but bare stone, a broken arch, the ordinary night beyond. But when he switched over his brown eye saw the colours and the candles but his blue eye saw, where the throne had been, nothing.

Only one thing did not change. Whichever way he chose to look he kept seeing in the corner of both eyes a sort of shadow, but with nothing solid to cast it, a sort of place where somehow the room did not seem to fit with itself.

He was looking at *Her* with his brown eye when she rose, smiling at Fara.

"Welcome," she said. "Farabinellabinillabefarrabellilla, most beautiful child that ever was or will be born in all my lands."

The smiling lips were very red now, the small teeth white and sharp, and the little tongue flickered between them. She turned her gaze on Dan and frowned.

"And you, boy, you are far from welcome. The most hideous child that ever was or will be born. What are you doing in my castle?"

Dan stood tongue-tied.

"You poor boy. I cannot bear to look at you like that."

She came towards Dan, seeming to move in a haze of marvellous odours, Maytime and fresh bread and ploughland after rain, bitter woodsmoke, the sharp herbs used in sickness, wild honey, old wine, drowning his mind, holding him still. She put the centre finger of her left hand to her mouth and licked it with her curled red tongue, then gently touched his left eye and his right.

His squint was gone.

In that bewildering instant, as the two sightlines clicked together, he was looking not at the enchantress but over her left shoulder. There hung the strange shadow he had so far seen only out of the corner of his eyes, the first thing he had ever looked at with both of them at the same time, a black blob, floating there, not part of the rich room at all, not fitting, roughly the shape of a frog.

"Look at me," said the enchantress.

Dan did as he was told. Now she no longer shifted her shape, but stayed the same woman, the bloodless queen with the sunken cheeks and the red wet lips.

"That is better," she said. "I can bear to look at you now. You will never be handsome so you may as well be useful. Go and sit at the table and learn from my old man how to keep my big book, so that when he dies you can take his place."

She turned to Fara and stretched out a hand with ivory fingers and scarlet nails an inch long.

"Come, child," she whispered. "I am ready for you now."

Fara's arm fell from Dan's waist, but he kept his own firm and held her close.

"No," he said.

She turned. Her eyes in the hollows of her skull flashed bright with fury.

Dan stared back, unafraid.

"You do not know my name," he said.

"Something too short and stupid to be troubled with. Let go, or you will suffer as nobody has ever suffered before."

"I know your name," said Dan. "I know your name, and you do not. You do not know your own name."

Now she hesitated, edging a little away, still holding her hand out to Fara but looking at Dan. Fara did not try to follow her.

"There is one syllable of your name you do not know," said Dan. "It is covered with a blot in the book. It is my name. Because your name is all the names in the book. All our names. You are us. You are our dream. You are our nightmare."

She swung and faced him, arms half spread with the pale palms towards him, an old woman, frail and pleading.

"You exist because we suppose you to exist," said Dan. "Now I suppose you not to."

There was a moment like the stopping of a heart, then all light vanished. A wail, dwindling to a far sigh. Blackness.

Fara and Dan, holding each other close, waited, trembling a little until the blackness cleared and they found themselves bathed in moonlight, standing in the centre of a roofless old hall, with the broken battlements of a castle all around them.

They walked up the village street in the dawn, still holding each other close. Fara's mother, sweeping her doorstep, looked up and saw them.

"Who are you?" she asked.

"We are Fara and Dan."

"I do not know you."

Dan's father, driving his donkey out to fetch hay, met them.

"Who are you?" he asked.

"We are Fara and Dan."

"I do not know you."

Other villagers, starting their day's work, gathered to stare. They saw a blonde girl, pretty but not amazingly so, and a dark boy, plain but not distressingly so. The girl's eyes were clear blue, but the boy's were greyish, flecked here and there with blue and brown.

"We've been to *Her* castle," said the children. "Now *She* has gone for ever. Look."

The villagers turned to see. Yes, there lay the wood, with ordinary oaks and beeches, and ordinary brambles beneath. Above the tree-tops in a cloudless sky rose broken towers, the ruins of some old castle built for forgotten wars. The villagers stared at the children with unfriendly eyes.

"We do not know you," they said. "You do not belong here. Go away."

So Fara and Dan left and found work in another country and did well and married people of that country but stayed neighbours and friends all their lives. In their old country the farmers went about their work as usual by day, but in the evenings they muttered together round their hearths and at night they dreamed their dreams. Slowly, fed on those mutterings and dreams, the trees of the wood grew dense and huge, and the brambles thickened beneath them and the green snakes bred again among the stems. Then the castle rebuilt itself and the clouds drifted between its turrets and pinnacles, and *She* came back to live there as before, to keep field and farm rich but taking the beautiful children as her price, sending for them when it was time, whatever their parents did to stop them, so that one day they stole down to the wood and were lost.

But never again was any child born as beautiful as Farabinellabinilla-befarrabellilla, or as hideous as Dan. *She* took care of that.

Years, centuries pass. The rock does not change, but the moor round it changes. Each winter the grass withers, each spring the heather makes small green leaves, like scales, and sheds the leaves it made last spring. The dead grass-blades and leaves rot down, become earth, feeding the new growth above them. So the moor rises in fractions of an inch, a slow green tide, until it covers the last lichened ridge of the great rock. Now, if you crossed the moor, you would not know that the rock was there.

It is, and so is he. But now when he wakes he does not know for sure he is awake. So much of his life has been dreams, so much of his memory is his own imaginings piled layer on layer on older imaginings, like the moor above. Memories of memories, the assassin-priest at the well, the glittering knights at the ford, old dreams feeding fresh dreams . . .

... DREAMS

WOLVES in the roadways, brothers at war,
  The sword a tool to be bought and sold,
Savages raiding the eastern shore
           And the King old, old.

"Newest of all my knights, now ride,
  Quarter my kingdom, search moor and fell.
Find me the mage who stood at my side
           When the world was well."

A crazed knight dodders across the hills
  Blear-eyed, mumbling and listening at stones.
His armour is rusted away. He feels
           Ice in his bones.

The last King lies in a secret grave.
  His Caer is sacked and his kingdom gone
Under the savages' conquering wave.
           But the search goes on.

Where? Which outcrop on what blank moor?
  They swore there was something that could not die.
It might sleep, but would wake when needed . . . Or
           Is it all a lie?

On a cliff which the ravens swoop beneath
  (He does not see them, but hears their calls)
He lies exhausted and waits for death.
           Mild sunlight falls

On limbs and turf . . . There is something there,
  Not heard like the calling birds, but felt . . .
A presence filling the tingling air,
           Seeming to melt

Times into Time . . . In this Time, this Place
A boy lies watching the ravens' flight,
Not outside, but filling the self-same space
As the dying knight . . .

And others whose times are still to be
Here in this instant, layer within layer,
Mind within mind, like the rings of a tree
Grown fresh each year

Till it holds the centuries, age within age . . .
The last knight dies in the evening dew
Knowing the tale of the sleeping mage
Was a lie, but true.

Nowhere, ever, for him to find
Under any boulder on moor or hill
But buried in minds fresh born that mind
Dreams on, dreams still.